Tempestuous

Tempestuous

Kim Askew and Amy Helmes

MeritPress

F+W Media, Inc.

Published by Merit Press
an imprint of F+W Media, Inc.
10151 Carver Road, Suite 200
Blue Ash, Ohio 45242
www.meritpressbooks.com

ISBN 10: 1-4405-5264-9
ISBN 13: 978-1-4405-5264-9
eISBN 10: 1-4405-5265-7
eISBN 13: 978-1-4405-5265-6

Printed in the United States of America.

10 9 8 7 6 5 4 3 2 1

This book is available at quantity discounts for bulk purchases.
For information, please call 1-800-289-0963.

How Camest Thou in This Pickle?

The handcuffs chafed my wrist, but that was nothing compared with the irritation I felt regarding the cretin to whom I was currently shackled.

I finally broke my silence, not with a word but with an—"Ow!"

"Jeez, Miranda, what now?"

"Would you stop yanking your arm around for two seconds?"

"I barely moved!"

"It's like you have Tourette's or something. My god!"

Caleb directed his green-grey eyes at me in a flash of annoyance.

"Listen, princess—I'm not enjoying this any more than you are. Now let's think." He shifted his glance to the towering cardboard boxes surrounding us. "There's got to be some way out of here."

"For the record, I don't think the psycho who locked us in here conveniently left an escape route for us to find. By the way, if you call me princess again, I *will* scream."

"At least maybe someone would hear us in here and let us out. Anyway, I thought you're the one who's supposed to have all the answers. Can't you wave your magic mascara wand and conjure us out of here?"

"Very funny. Sorry, but being handcuffed to your ass for the last six hours has robbed me of my powers—not to mention my will to live. And don't think I wouldn't kill to have some mascara right about now. I'm sure I look like a hot mess."

"Quite the opposite, actually." His unforeseen compliment threw me off guard. Flustered, I redoubled my efforts at cynicism, shifting awkwardly on the cold cement floor.

"With my luck, there are rats lurking around here somewhere. Maybe they can chew through these handcuffs and liberate me. I still cannot believe we don't have the key."

"We're not having this conversation again."

I sighed and shifted uncomfortably on my butt bones.

"What's wrong now?"

"Nothing. My back hurts." Caleb abruptly leaned away from me and started rooting in the corner of the storeroom, as far as he could reach, with his one free hand. Just as I was about to blast him again for jerking me around, he hoisted up a clear plastic garbage bag filled with Styrofoam packing peanuts. This he proceeded to wedge behind my back like a makeshift beanbag chair.

"Better?" He made a few adjustments as I nodded, unwilling to acknowledge his act of chivalry. I rested my hands in my lap, letting his right hand—manacled to my left—graze my outer thigh. Ordinarily, I wouldn't have tolerated such close physical proximity from a guy like Caleb, but in one short night, he and I had already been through an extraordinary saga of events. I leaned in to touch my shoulder to his as the reality of the situation sunk in.

"Caleb?"

"Yeah?"

"I'm scared." Without looking at me, or saying a word, he rotated his wrist to clutch my hand in his. It was strong and guitar-calloused, and I knew that it was my one saving grace in this absurdly surreal night. At least we were in this together.

CHAPTER ONE

Hang Not on My Garments

Singing along to the latest overplayed indie rock tune pulsing from the stereo speakers, I pulled my car into a spot at the far end of the parking lot reserved for mall employees and then let it idle, dragging out my last few minutes in the cocooning warmth. The song ended and the deejay's grating baritone voice kicked in:

> *"That was the latest from a local group, the Drunk Butlers. We're interrupting this music marathon to let you know about a winter storm advisory in effect for tonight, lasting until five A.M. tomorrow morning. Bundle up! It's going to be a B-R-R-R-R-utal one tonight! Grab someone hot to keep you warm, and we'll keep things real with more nonstop hits comin' atcha."*

Snowflakes the size of quarters drifted onto my windshield as I contemplated the slushy expanse between my vehicle and the mall's main entrance. I could think of about a million other things I'd rather be doing on a Saturday night than working a five-hour shift serving lukewarm hot dogs to mall rats before driving home in possibly blizzard-like conditions. Unless I literally broke a leg—I wistfully imagined slipping on the ice and being rescued by a cute EMT—there was just no getting around it. I reached into the backseat and grabbed the ridiculously tall, absurdly colorful hat I was forced to wear as part of my Hot-Dog Kabob uniform. Sadly, my recent fall from grace and subsequent mandated employment had coincided with a lack of decent part-time jobs. I'd at least hoped to be spritzing perfume from behind a beauty counter at one of the department stores or playing hostess at the "high-end" chain restaurant Teasers, on the other end of the mall, but all the less-humiliating positions were already taken—so I was resigned to looking like an escaped circus lunatic in head-to-toe garish blue-and-yellow stripes. Have I mentioned the worst part? The fake plastic wiener that sits atop the hat, spinning on an axis? It's basically a fashionista's worst nightmare come to life, but try telling that to my dad . . . or the school superintendent who insisted I take a job as part of my "reparations." I sighed deeply, turned off the engine, and wrapped my coat tightly around me.

Stepping gingerly out of the car, I lowered the towering hat onto my head and, shivering, pinned it into place with bobby pins from my coat pocket. I usually waited until the very last second to don this monstrosity, but frankly (pun intended) it was just too damn cold to go without it. I looked to the right and left, hoping no one was observing me. As I glanced behind me, I was startled to see someone standing behind the car.

A creepy-looking guy in a long black wool overcoat stood about six feet away, staring at me. I self-consciously realized that my hot-dog propeller must have been spinning in the wind, and I flushed, as if I'd just been caught with my pants at half-mast. Damn this hat! But still, it was seriously rude of him to stare. I glanced again, and he was still standing there—tall and broad-shouldered, with a mass of thick black hair. I couldn't see his eyes, which were shrouded by a furry cap, but he couldn't have been older than twenty. Snowflakes were collecting on his shoulders—or was that just colossal dandruff? His coat hung open, revealing faded black jeans and bulky black boots. An indistinguishable piece of black fabric hung limply from his fist. As if bored, he slowly turned on his heel and lumbered toward the mall entrance. Whatever, loser!

I clicked my key fob to lock the door and started off across the wintry expanse of the parking lot. The howling wind swirled around me. I shrieked and placed one hand on top of my hat, lest the propeller somehow succeed in lifting me up off the ground. Small eddies of snow spiraled at my feet on the blacktop, but I walked in baby steps, not wanting to fall on a slick patch. The regulation navy blue sneakers I was wearing offered zero traction. Shivering, I wrapped my down parka closer to my torso, but my legs were freezing, clad only in bright red tights under a polyester, royal-blue-and-yellow-striped jumper. The wind stung my face and brought tears to my eyes. At least, I think it was the wind causing me to well up. I thought about this time last month, when I might have come to the mall only to supplement my wardrobe or hang out with my friends, not to shovel greasy food across a counter at people who seriously needed to rethink their carb intake.

Brian Bishop was to blame for all of this. Correction: Brian along with the girls *formerly* known as my best friends—Rachel, Britney, and Whitney. I scowled thinking about them and tried to avoid stepping in the big piles of gray, wet slush near the curb. My life had metaphorically turned to slush in recent weeks, and I held them personally responsible.

Approaching the entrance, I recognized a faux-deputy uniform on the other side of the glass door. It belonged to Grady Pfeiffer, a member of the mall's Keystone Cop security team. He looked unnerved as he glanced out at the snow, but when he saw me, he threw me a chipper nod and leaned on the door to open it for me.

"Thanks," I said, already exhausted and chilled to the bone.

"Afternoon, Miranda. Cold enough for you, huh?" Stamping my feet to get a bit of feeling back in them, I wasn't in the mood for his congenial chit-chat, but he failed to take notice. "How are things?"

"My life is a complete cataclysm, but thanks for asking," I grumbled as I walked past him into the mall.

"Well, uh. . . ." He was stymied by my dose of attitude, and since I wasn't inclined to elaborate on my troubles I decided to issue a momentary gag order on my grousing. Grady hadn't done anything to deserve it, after all.

"Just kidding. I'm freezing my ass off, but other than that I'm fine. Really."

"Well, that's good," he said, joining me as I trudged on toward my destination. "Not for your, er, ass, I mean, but well . . . uhh . . . you know I'm always here to help. . . ."

"Thanks, Grady, I know." I flashed him one of my famous smiles, guaranteed to melt butter. "Oh, actually—there *is* one teensy, tiny thing you can do for me. . . ." I paused dramatically. I normally tried not to abuse my power on people as defenseless as Grady, but every once in a while I had to flex my muscles.

"Anything! If it's something the law and the sweet Lord above allows of course." He blushed to the roots of his brown hair, which was close-cropped, military-style.

"My request is innocent enough, I can assure you. It's Ariel's birthday, and I want to surprise her after work with an ice cream cake from Just Desserts. Think you can swing by and pick it up for me on your rounds a few minutes before nine? I can pay you later," I added, feeling up to adjust my idiotic chapeau. The Hot-Dog Kabob refrigerator was crammed full of frozen wieners and some rubbery pasteurized processed cheese—I didn't want a perfectly good mint-chip cake getting tainted by being stored in the same fetid freezer space.

"Weeellllll," Grady drew out the word as if it contained five syllables, shifted on his heels, then concluded the performance with a broad wink, "I'm really not supposed to do anything like that while I'm on duty. But for you, I'll make an exception." It wasn't as if I was asking him to *steal* the cake for god's sake, but Grady was a tad obsessed with "protocol." We were both relatively new employees here, but unlike yours truly, he couldn't take his job more seriously if he were guarding the perimeter at Fort Knox.

I thanked the rent-a-cop and headed past Treasure Hunt Antiques & Collectibles and its display window full of creepy china dolls, rare coins, and mint-condition baseball cards. I poked my head in to look for Mike, the store clerk who usually worked this shift, but he wasn't at his usual spot behind the counter. Next door was Hair Apparent, the mall's only salon with its attached Glamour Puss portrait studio. No matter how many times I passed by, I never failed to snort with derision at the decade-old display photos meant to entice middle-aged moms to doll-up like models for their hubbies. The women were plastered with makeup and wrapped in feather boas like a bad Vegas act, wrinkly cleavage spilling out of low-cut sequined gowns.

"Miranda! Miss Fabulous!" Alfredo burst from Hair Apparent and traipsed toward me for a hug and a swoopy air kiss on the cheek. Dressed to the nines as usual, he sported a purple tie and matching sweater vest. "Check out the cufflinks," he said, holding out his arm for inspection. "They're mermaids." The boy did have exquisite, if colorful, taste.

"Nice," I said admiringly. "Hey, I'm throwing a surprise birthday party for Ariel after we close tonight. Can you come by?"

"I don't know," he said, pushing his long, razored bangs out of his face. "I have a scorchingly hot date tonight."

"Stop by, *pleeease,* and you can have the challenge of a lifetime—giving Ariel a makeover," I wheedled.

"Well, you know I can't pass up the chance to turn that duckling into a swan. I'll swing by, but just for a few minutes. How old is the tiny thing, anyway? Twelve?"

I made a face.

"She's turning seventeen and you know it. Oh, by the way, I was going to ask Mike, too, but it looks like he's on his break. Can you let him know for me?"

"Sure thing." Alfredo sauntered back inside Hair Apparent and I continued my forced march down the wide hallway. The piped-in easy listening tunes were already giving me a killer headache, and I could hear the faint screeching of kids at the Cheeze Monkey pizzeria/arcade on the other side of the mall. Oh well, I thought optimistically, at least I'm not working again until Tuesday night. I mentally added up the amount I'd make tonight. Five hours of work equaled just about forty-two bucks—it would barely make a dent in what I was expected to pay back in restitution. Back when I'd had an allowance, fifty dollars had been chump change, approximately what I'd spend on a sushi lunch during a shopping spree with my friends. My former friends, that is.

I wondered, a tad wistfully, what Rachel and the "Itneys" were doing today. Probably planning their annual winter ski trip to Aspen or breaking in matching pairs of whatever high-priced boots *Vogue* deemed "must-have" this season. They didn't have a care in the world that their daddies' AmEx cards couldn't fix. As shallow as it sounded, sometimes I wished I could still say the same.

CHAPTER TWO

O Brave New World

I hung a right at the corner by the Bead Bungalow and headed toward the escalator leading down to the food court. Like the Greek goddess Persephone, I was constantly forced to return to this underworld. A garishly painted plaster arch curved ominously around the escalators as though it were the very mouth of hell. The smell of grease wafting up triggered my gag reflex.

"Hey, Miranda, wait up!" My coworker Ariel's chirpy voice interrupted my fleeting sense of nausea as she half skipped up beside me, her matching uniform hat swaying level with my shoulder. I teasingly flicked her hot dog propeller and sent it spinning. A gung-ho grin spread across her perky face and revealed the astonishing shimmer of orthodontia, which caused her to speak with a breathy lisp. Ariel's brown hair curled around her face in waves, and her cheeks were always rosy, as if she was in a constant state of having just finished a ten-yard dash. At a diminutive five-foot-two, she reminded me of a mischievous pixie. She was still wearing a pair of mittens, which were attached to her coat cuffs by Hello Kitty clips.

"Don't you love the snow? I love the snow!" she as good as squealed. "Snow angels and snowmen and snowball fights and snow forts and snow angels and. . . ."

"Stop! What are you, like, seven?" I remembered Alfredo's earlier quip about her childish nature.

"As a matter of fact, today's my. . . ."

"Your birthday. I know. You don't have to remind me."

"I just love that it's snowing on my birthday. It's like getting the whole world covered with the universe's magic birthday frosting!" Oh boy. At times, Ariel's naively chipper disposition grated on my nerves. Her boundless enthusiasm and my healthy sarcasm went together about as well as a helium balloon and a bucket of rusty nails. Then again, her happy-go-lucky attitude had singlehandedly propped up my defeatist one during the duration of my always-hellish shifts. And given that she wasn't exactly up to speed on my recent academic offenses, it was actually somewhat refreshing to be in her nonjudgmental presence. Truth be told, the girl kind of idolized me, and I knew it.

"Because it's your birthday, and *only* because it's your birthday, I won't make you drain and clean out the fryer."

"But you hate doing that." Ariel looked astonished. "Toxic sludge, you called it. You'd do that for me?"

"I didn't say *I'm* going to do it! We'll just, you know . . . conveniently forget! Let Sunday's crew deal with it."

Ariel's eyes widened gleefully, as if we'd just hatched a plan to rob the Louvre.

"You think we can?"

"Of course!"

"Wait. . . ." she seemed confused. "Aren't I your manager?"

"Semantics." Ariel had been working at Hot-Dog Kabob for about nine months, which technically made her my supervisor when we worked shifts together. But we both knew who was really running the show. *C'est moi.*

As we hopped on the escalator and started our descent, I glanced over at Got Games and noticed a guy standing just outside the shop. Where had I seen him before? Oh yeah. The creep from the parking lot! I almost didn't recognize him because he was now wearing a stupid black sorcerer's cape with glittery crescent moons emblazoned upon it. Given his brooding stance, he could have been mistaken for a bar bouncer or a Secret Service agent. What a ridiculous getup, I scoffed, before it occurred to me that I had absolutely no room to talk. I pulled my back straighter and held my head up trying to project a sense of dignity while simultaneously avoiding eye contact. I could tell he was staring at me again.

"What's with the Hogwarts dropout over there?" I mumbled to Ariel, out of the corner of my mouth. She immediately whipped her head in the direction of my gaze. "Don't look!" I said with a groan. "He'll know we're talking about him!"

"Well, how am I supposed to know who you're talking about if I don't look?"

"Just don't be obvious about it." I craned my head in the opposite direction.

"Okay, you can relax," she said, "Caleb can't see us anymore."

"Caleb? You know him?"

"Yes, he started last month, too, which you would know if you'd pay attention to what was going on around here. You're kind of self-obsessed, you know?" Did I mention that Ariel was also whip-smart and totally called me on my shit? She was the only one who could.

"Whatever. He's clearly a degenerate, in any case," I shrugged.

Ariel shook her head as if in protest. "He's really nice! Last week he helped me find a copy of the new *Unicorn Fantasy III* game."

"Okay, as if you needed anymore geek credentials," I said. "Hey, maybe he's your match made in avatar heaven! I can see where he might clean up okay."

"Miranda!" Ariel emitted an embarrassed squeal. "Nooo! He's so not my type."

"You have a type?" I wondered, curious now. We stepped off the escalator and headed in the glaringly fluorescent-lit direction of the food court, leaving oafish gamer boy in our wake.

Expert matchmaker that I was, I would have liked to press Ariel for more details regarding her ideal mate, but as we approached the throng of tables and chairs arrayed in the center of the food court, I was silenced by the multitude of angry stares aimed in my direction.

Normally chatty, Ariel didn't breathe a word; meaning she'd noticed it, too. Let's just say my high school classmates hadn't been very subtle in their scorn ever since I'd been busted a little more than a month ago. My crime? Running a secret online matching service that paid geeks to tutor athletes and other scholastic underachievers—all for a small commission fee, of course. It had seemed innocent enough at the time. The dumb jocks got passing grades, and the geeks made a tidy profit. How was I to know it would turn into a massive cheating scam? I stared straight ahead as we walked passed Paisano's Pizza-by-the-Slice and Fro-Yo-Yo frozen yogurt, trying not to let my face show how pained I was to have become my high school's pariah. *This* was the thanks I got for trying to help people! Was it my fault that their college apps were now dead in the water because of the disciplinary storm that had ensued?

"Nice hat," said an epidermally challenged junior, Stacy Scott, who was refilling her Diet Coke from Taco Corner's soft-drink machine. Wow, really creative insult, I mused, giving her a tight, cynical smile.

Out of the corner of my eye, I saw Reggie Williams dunk his chicken nugget in a massive pile of ketchup. He waved the sauce-soaked morsel of processed meat over his head.

"Hey, Miranda," he said with a sneer as his friends grinned devilishly. "Have you managed to 'catch up' yet? Or should I say . . . *pay* up?" (School officials had demanded that I pay back the entire $3,920 that I had earned from my little enterprise.) Kids at a few other tables echoed more profane and equally idiotic sentiments that I pretended not to hear.

I noticed Ariel dart me a sideways glance as we hurried along toward Hot-Dog Kabob, and I ignored her imploring, concerned eyes. I threw open the hinged counter separating the customers from the employees, chucked my purse on the shelf under the stack of Styrofoam cups, and raced to the grim, closet-sized bathroom. Slamming the door, I leaned my head against it, no longer concerned about whether or not I was mussing my bangs in the process. Giant tears started to pool in the bottom rims of my eyes, and my face flushed hot.

It could have been worse, I told myself. Brian, Rachel, and the Itneys could have been out there throwing me their accusatory bullshit, as if I'd started this whole mess in the first place.

After about a minute, my breathing had returned to normal. Not being the sort of chick who'd hide out in the bathroom all evening rather than face her detractors, I wet a paper towel and dabbed my cheeks, cursing the fact that there was no mirror in which to check my eye makeup. Hopefully I wasn't too raccooned-out. I fake flushed the toilet, ran the faucet once more, took a deep breath, and reemerged hopefully looking cool as a cucumber. Couldn't let 'em think I'd been bested.

"Hot-diggity-dog!" I said, returning to the counter with a businesslike smile on my face. I grabbed my apron and tossed Ariel a package of wooden skewers. Relieved that I wasn't down for the count, Ariel flashed me a metallic grin and returned to her post. I slid a giant bucket of lemons across the counter and began slicing them in half for the lemonade press. Only four hours and fifty minutes to go.

CHAPTER THREE

What a Spendthrift Is He of His Tongue

I took my sweet-ass time on the lemon-halving, so that the food-court's high-strung supervisor, Randall Bauer, wouldn't put me to work manning the dreaded fryer. Just then, as if conjured from the deep, the whale of a man sauntered over on his two chubby legs. He yanked at his clip-on tie, which came off in one gesture. Under his other arm, he clutched a down parka, ski cap, and bulky hand-knit scarf, ridiculously over-prepared for the simple trek to his car.

"Ariel, Miranda—I'm heading home now before the roads get too iffy. I trust you two girls can hold down the fort this evening?"

"Sure thing, Randy," I replied, knowing he hated the shortened version of his name. He raised his eyebrows and glanced at me.

"You," he pointed. "I don't want to get another complaint from management saying you're serving food without your hat. It violates the health code."

"Won't happen again," I swore with a diffident smile. He harrumphed once, cleared his throat, then pivoted to go on his way when I called him back.

"Speaking of health. . . ." Randall sighed and glanced at his watch. "I was thinking maybe it would be a good idea to consider offering some healthy alternatives to the food court menu. It's like we're in the fast-food Dark Ages. I mean, even McDonald's has salads and yogurt these days."

"Miranda," he said. "Trust me, we're giving the people what they want. And what they want is pizza, hot dogs, and something a little exotic—like stir-fry."

"Stir-fry is hardly exotic. What about organic, local, fair-trade? Don't those words mean *anything* to you?"

"Ever consider moving to California?" He changed the subject, reminding me that I needed to get some more dogs out of the walk-in freezer. If Randall thought the argument was over, he had another thing coming. My powers of persuasion would ultimately wear him down.

After retrieving more hot dogs from the back and placing them in the fridge under the counter to thaw, I stared out at the deserted dining area of the food court and realized the futility of my errand. "There's no way we're going to need these," I pointed out to Ariel.

"It is pretty dead today," she agreed.

"It's the weather. Everyone's staying home. And with Randall gone. . . ."

"What are you saying?" Even someone as artless as Ariel could tell I was up to something.

"Well, when the cat's away, the mice are obligated to play. Or at least slack off a little."

Thirty minutes later, Ariel and I sat cross-legged on the counter in our jumpers and sneakers—health code be damned!—using frozen hot dogs to play our own jimmy-rigged version of Jenga. As I concentrated on liberating a loose hot dog from the bottom of the stack without letting the precarious tower come crashing down, Ariel gave me the third degree about high school life.

"So, do you get to decorate your locker however you like?"

"Uh. Yeah, I guess."

"God, you're soooo lucky!" she sighed.

"Seriously, Ariel, it's not that great. *You're* the one living the charmed life."

"What, because I'm homeschooled? If being trapped all day with your *MOM* is considered cool these days then, yeah, I guess."

"But you get to just hang out at your house all day."

"You make it sound like a vacation! It's more like prison! With my mom as the warden!"

"I'd give anything to spend some time with my mother."

Ariel seemed cowed, but not necessarily convinced. "The worst thing about not getting to go to a real high school is that I'm so *out* of it," she continued. "How can I ever be cool or have any friends if I don't even know what the cool kids are like? It's like being on a deserted island or something. No prom, no pep rallies . . . I'm so out of the loop."

"For the record, it's not even cool to use the word 'cool,'" I explained. "Besides, the loop's not all that. In fact, it's a real minefield." As I said the words, something out of the corner of my eye caused me to startle, which sent the entire tower of frosty frankfurters crashing down onto the counter.

"Playing with your food again, are we?" Oh no. Not *him.*

"Caleb!" Ariel jumped off the counter and used the back of her forearm to sweep all the frozen hot dogs into the garbage can.

"Uh, hey there," he muttered back. "How's the video game working out?"

"I reached the third level of Lavender City two nights ago!" Ariel reported proudly. "I'm still trying to find the glitter key to unlock Pegasus from his moonbeam cage." She may as well have been speaking Geek Chinese, but apparently Caleb could decipher it.

"I don't know that game well," he said, glancing at me as if to prove his manliness, "but I think the key for that level is hidden in one of the secret thoroughfares."

"The Misty Tulip Passage?" Ariel sounded fascinated.

"Could be. That sounds familiar." I vaguely understood what Ariel meant when she said Caleb wasn't her type. There was something dark, even surly about him. Watching him try to discuss *Unicorn Fantasy III* was like watching a vampire politely attempt to eat people food, especially since he was still wearing that stupid cape. My coworker made the obligatory introductions.

"Caleb, this is Miranda; Miranda, Caleb."

"Charmed, I'm sure." (Though I wasn't. Not in the slightest.)

"So you guys haven't met before?" Ariel asked.

"I'm not sure I've had the pleasure," he answered. I decided to spare us both the mortification of mentioning our little *tête-à-tête* in the parking lot earlier, but the smirk on his face as he stared at me suggested he hadn't forgotten.

"You want to order something? Can I entice you with a frankfurter impaled on a wooden stake?"

"After watching you play Lincoln Logs with the merchandise, uh, no thank you."

"It's a good thing you showed up when you did," laughed Ariel. "Miranda was on her way to winning the fourth Jenga match in a row. She's got really nimble fingers." Uggh. I would have to counsel Ariel later about making stupid comments.

"Some power," Caleb marveled.

"I mainly use it for good, but consider yourself forewarned," I deadpanned.

"Oh my God!!!" Ariel shrieked from behind me, as if she'd just witnessed a murder.

"What?!?"

"We're running low on mustard."

"WTF, Ariel, the fact hardly merits such a spasmodic freak-out."

"But I don't want to run out if we get busy later. I'll go get more from the stockroom." She disappeared into the back of the store like a flash of lightning, leaving me alone with Mr. Wonderful.

"She's a bit . . . frenetic, huh?" he finally ventured.

"You noticed?"

"Almost gave me whiplash the first time I met her. The girl's got energy to spare. She's cute, though." Cute? Hold the phone! Maybe Ariel was *his* type! Only one way to find out. Let the matchmaking prowess begin.

"So, what are you doing when the mall closes tonight?" I asked in my trademarked, charm-the-pants-off-'em voice. Caleb's eyes narrowed and he cocked his head slightly in response to my question.

"Tonight? Um . . . I sort of have plans already." He said this apologetically, as if he were letting me down gently. Oh. Wait a minute. Did he think *I* was asking *him* out? For the second time today he caused me to flush with embarrassment.

"It's just that some of us are getting together at nine tonight to celebrate Ariel's birthday," I hurried to explain. "She's turning seventeen. Thought you might want to swing by for a piece of cake."

"Ohhhh." His face might have turned red, too, but it was hard to tell with the way his hair cascaded over half of it. "Well, as it turns out, I sort of have to be somewhere after work and it's kind of important. But hey, thanks for asking."

Great. So this *cretin*, in addition to being vain enough to think I had the hots for him, was too busy, no—make that self-involved—to stop by for five minutes for Ariel's sake? How rude.

"Well, don't mention anything to her about it when she comes back. It's a surprise." Saying this, I came across sounding more dejected than I meant to. I could hear the tinkle of Ariel's bell earrings getting closer, and was glad I wouldn't have to make small talk for much longer. Ariel dropped the gallon-sized container of Heinz mustard on the counter and was about to refill the pump dispenser when the phone rang shrilly in the back room.

"I'll get iiit!" my coworker announced in a sing-song voice, and before I could even protest, she was gone again in a flash.

"So, guess I'll see you around. . . ." I said bluntly to Caleb, willing him to leave my presence.

"Sure. But actually . . . I just remembered a trick for Ariel about that video game she bought. So I'll just wait till she comes back." Greeeaaat. Captain Caveman and I stared blankly at one another for a few moments until I could think of something else to say.

"You sell video games?"

"Yeah. All sorts of games, actually, board games, puzzles . . . you know the drill."

"No, actually, I don't. So what's with the cape? Is that some sort of Dungeons & Dragons nod or are you just a tragic slave to fashion?"

"Standard-issue uniform. We sell magic paraphernalia, too."

"Oh, right. Magic." I said this with as much boredom in my voice as I could muster. Another awkward silence ensued, but this time I decided not to try and fill it. I pretended to check the condiments and shuffled various items around until Caleb finally spoke up.

"Soooo, you go to Eastern Prep, right?"

"Yep." I braced for some snide comment about my recent fall from grace, and was surprised when it never materialized.

"I'll graduate from Marshall this year," he said. Public school. Explains why we'd never crossed paths before, and why he seemed to know most of the other food court employees. More silence. "So, how long have you been working here?"

"Feels like ten years, but it's only been twenty-eight days, one hour and," I stopped to check the clock on the wall behind me, "forty-seven minutes."

"I know what you mean."

"Wouldn't most gamer types kill to stand around swapping stories about level advancement, virtual weaponry, and crap like that?"

"I'm not a gamer. And I wouldn't be caught dead anywhere near this capitalist bullshit if I didn't need the money."

I heard a noise behind me as Ariel came from the back room, clearing her throat loudly. "So, you two are chattin' it up. That's great!" she said. I rolled my eyes at her, but she didn't seem to notice. "Guess what?" She looked at us expectantly.

"The chase: cut to it, Ariel." I knew from experience that she could drag out a guessing game forever if given any encouragement whatsoever.

"Oh alright. My mom just called and she said the storm is getting *way* worse."

"So?"

"Sooo, maybe we'll get snowed in!"

"Yeah, gee, *that* would be *fantastic*," I said, not hiding the sarcasm. "Trapped in the mall all night. We probably wouldn't even get paid for it."

"Wait, you don't think it could really happen?" Ariel looked from Caleb's face to mine, suddenly concerned. "Mom has my birthday dinner all planned. . . ."

"Don't worry," Caleb said. "The weather reporters always exaggerate this stuff—makes for a better story."

"Yeah," I said. "The next thing you know they'll be calling it the 'White Death' and CNN will have a special logo and soundtrack for it."

Caleb gave me an appreciative nod.

"Exactly. Well, I'd better get back before they send a search party. See you later. By the way, Ariel, I remember reading in the sales manual for *UFIII* that the red flowers in the Tulip Passage are poisonous. So heads up on that."

"Gee, thanks!" Ariel beamed. Sales manual. Righhht.

When he was out of earshot, I turned back to my coworker only to find her staring at me with a knowing expression.

"What?" I asked her.

"Soooo. . . ." she said, "What do you think?"

"He's alright. He may or may not be hiding a unibrow with those long bangs, but at least he seems to have a sense of humor. How long have you been crushing on him?"

"*Me?*" she said wonderingly. "What are you talking about?"

"Whatever, Miss Coy, if you don't want to talk about it, we don't have to. I'm not going to twist your arm." I leaned with my back against the counter and looked at her smugly. "Anyway, what should we do now? We could play fashion designer and each create an outfit using only supplies from the stockroom."

"Actually," Ariel's face turned somber as she glanced over my left shoulder. "I think we might have some customers."

I slowly turned to face out toward the food court and my heart stopped cold, midbeat. The Four Horsemen of the Apocalypse would have been a preferred alternative to the group that stood before me.

CHAPTER FOUR

Good Wombs Have Borne Bad Sons

I grabbed both sides of the cash register and braced myself for a verbal pummeling.

"Wow, Miranda, the 'minimum-wage look' really suits you," Rachel sneered, eyeing me from head to toe. Whitney and Britney, snickering into her shoulders like two loyal toadies, flanked her. Physically (and mentally) they resembled a triptych of Barbie dolls, each with a varying shade of unnaturally blonde locks. To their right, Brian Bishop, my ex—the equivalent of a brunette Ken—was texting into his phone, and I prayed he was too busy to give me the usual hate-filled glare. Typically, I was doomed to have no such luck.

"Well, well, well." He pocketed his cell and turned his attention to me. "If it isn't my enterprising former girlfriend. The one who cost me the Ivy League in addition to landing me in detention for the rest of the school year." The fact that Brian had needed to pay a proxy to write up a no-brainer, three-page paper on *The Scarlet Letter* was pretty strong evidence that he was never Yale material in the first place, but I refrained from pointing that out. I stared unflinchingly at my onetime love interest, wondering what I ever saw in him. In my peripheral vision, a fidgety Ariel waited nervously.

"Can I take your order?" I said, causing Rachel and the Itneys to erupt with laughter again.

"Miranda, why don't you, um, go get some mustard from the back?" Ariel suggested, a grim look on her normally cherubic face. Despite her bravado she resembled a playful kitten approaching a hungry pride of lions. I loved her for trying to spare me any further angst, but wasn't about to let her face this band of brigands alone.

"Thanks, Ariel, but I've got it."

"We didn't come by to order anything," Brian said. "We just wanted to say goodbye."

I looked at him quizzically. No goodbyes were necessary as far as I was concerned.

"We're leaving tomorrow for Aspen," Rachel leaned in faux confidingly. "And we'd invite you but—"

"You have to work." Britney and Whitney cackled in unison as if they were the evil stepsisters in some sort of low-budget adaptation of Cinderella.

"C'mon, guys—it smells like butt down here. Let's go ridicule Grady some more." Saying this, Rachel threw a possessive arm around Brian's shoulder. They turned away and headed toward the lower level's main thoroughfare: Main Street, as we employees called it. Only then did I let myself feel a twinge of jealousy. Whatever. I just had to make it through the rest of high school and then I could forget that these people ever existed.

"Miranda—" Ariel began.

"Thanks, but I don't want to talk about it." I held up my hand—palm out—in the universal symbol for *shut it.*

She and I spent the next hour-and-a-half twiddling our thumbs, for the most part. The clock seemed stuck on slo-mo thanks to our woeful lack of corn dog consumers. I finally sighed and untied my apron, tossing it to Ariel as if she were my valet.

"I'm going on my break."

I reached under the cash register for my copy of Jane Austen's *Emma* and prepared to head over to my "reserved" table on the far side of the food court hidden behind a strategically placed palm tree, part of the cafeteria's hokey tropical island–themed decor. (On a cold day like today the seashell-mosaic wall art and piped-in steel drum Calypso music seemed especially oxymoronic.) Right on cue, Derek from Fro-Yo-Yo approached the counter with the "Miranda Special," a vanilla frozen yogurt shake blended with fresh mint, honey, and chocolate chips.

"Here you go, Miranda," he said, blushing as he handed me the concoction. "Hope I put enough fresh mint in there this time."

"I'm sure it's delicious, Derek."

"Thanks. See you, um, later. . . ." He backed away, stumbling over his own feet in the process.

"You forgot to call her 'Your Highness,'" Ariel said under her breath. As I mentioned before, she wasn't afraid to call me on my shit. Okay, sure, maybe some of the mall employees tended to genuflect in my presence—at least the ones who didn't attend my school, like most of these food court geeks who hadn't heard about my recent scandal. It was only a matter of time before the gossip spread, but in the meantime, was it my fault if people took an instant liking to me? The evening was starting to look up. I smirked in Ariel's direction and made my way over to my table. I always looked forward to this part of the day. Not just because it was a break, but because it was when I felt most like I used to before everything fell apart.

I settled into my corner and opened my battered paperback, an old copy Mom had marked up in the margins during her college years. I was having a vacuum-cheeked, botched-facelift-victim moment trying to suck through a straw the thick shake Derek had brought me, so I set it aside to thaw for a bit. Most of the surrounding tables stood empty, detritus-covered red plastic trays dotting a few. It was almost time for the dinner rush but there was no sign of life in the fluorescent-lit food court. Two workers at Paisano's were perched on the counter playing rock-paper-scissors, and the dude that dished up stir-fry at Wok 'Dis Way looked pretty much catatonic. Come to think of it, we hadn't had any real customers all day. The mall was now dead.

Not that that was a bad thing. Like I said, most of the teenagers working at the mall attended surrounding public schools and were oblivious to my "crime of the century." On a slow night like this, I figured I wasn't likely to suffer any further oh-how-the-mighty-have-fallen moments.

Smoothing out a dog-eared fold in *Emma*, I sighed. My time would probably be better spent studying for chem class. I had an exam next Wednesday, but with all the drama I'd been wrapped up in over the past several weeks, schoolwork had not exactly been at the top of my priority list—especially since that's what had landed me in such deep shit in the first place. I felt my stomach churn as these unwelcome thoughts resurfaced from where I'd been trying to stow them away. It felt like herding errant cats: As much as I tried to rein them in, they wanted to escape and slink about my conscience, making mischief.

I tried hard to focus on the words in my book but it was no use. I was all at sea. How was I ever going to earn back all the money that was lost? How could such a good idea have gone so terribly wrong? Okay, so maybe what I'd done was not *technically* on the up-and-up, but my intentions had been one-hundred-percent pure! It seemed like such a win-win arrangement at the time, and after all, isn't arranging things what I did best? I was the girl who got things done: the "go-to" girl . . . wheeler-dealer . . . champion matchmaker, not to mention former homecoming queen. Now I was a first-class pariah with only a few out-of-the-loop, D-list mall employees for loyal subjects. I longed for the emotional equivalent of a life preserver like the ones that, alongside the fishing nets and anchors, festooned the food court's bright blue walls.

My restless thoughts kept pulling me back to the same infuriating question: What *had* I seen in Brian? Things had changed so much in the last few weeks that it was difficult to remember exactly what it had been like when we were together. Sure, I knew now that he'd double-crossed me, but there were moments when we'd really been in sync. Or so I'd thought! That's what hurt so much. I'd let down my guard in a way I hadn't with anyone since my mom died. Self-sufficiency was my creed, and I grew up fast, not just because she was gone, but because I knew my dad needed me to be strong for both of us. Brian had been the one to point out that my numerous do-gooder schemes and entrepreneurial ventures were likely prompted by a desire to wrest back control of my own destiny—and maybe to distract myself from the pain of losing her. I'd given him access to my previously impenetrable defenses. He'd made me trust him, then used it against me. How *could* I have been so stupid?

Managing, through sheer force of will, to keep my tears at bay, I suddenly spied at eye level a pair of too-tight black polyester shorts. I glanced up and saw a black-and-white-striped ref's jersey covering a vast swath of pectoral muscles. A blonde, blue-eyed chiseled face sat perched on a thick linebacker neck, around which hung a whistle. I didn't know this guy from Adam, but common sense told me he hailed from the Cleat Locker athletic apparel store on the other end of the mall, a location we food courtesans referred to as "Siberia."

I gazed up at this visitor quizzically, letting the words "jock strap" and "strapping jock" tumble playfully about my brain.

"Miranda, right?" the bronzed beefcake said with a stammer.

"Uh. Yeah?"

"Hi. You don't know me," he said, reaching for my right hand, which he proceeded to shake vigorously. "I'm Chad. Chad Mathers. I work down at the Cleat Locker."

"So I gathered." I eyed his white tube socks and black cross-trainers, hoping to god this was mandatory dress code and not the result of some ill-advised stylistic leanings. Not that I could talk with a hot dog perched on my head, but still.

"What can I do for you, Chad?" I sighed. He clearly wanted something. Guys like him always did.

"Well, I've been seeing you pass by the store and well, I was just curious. . . ." Of course. So, even though he must go to Marshall, he had heard all about the infamous Miranda Prospero and her scandalous blacklisting.

"Curious about what, Chad?" I was starting to get irritated. He flushed from the tip of his ears to his muscular knees.

"Just, I don't know, curious about who you are, I guess." For a varsity-type, he seemed less than stalwart in his approach. "I know you're friends with Ariel. She talks about you a lot. I guess I was just wondering, well, that is, if maybe one of these nights after work. . . . God, I'm really bad at this sort of thing. . . ." This was worse than I had imagined. Not only was he asking me out, but he was genuinely nervous! I could tell any cocky, rocks-for-brains jock to take his business elsewhere, but this guy was more like an overstuffed teddy bear with shaky self-confidence. Delicate maneuvering was in order here. I took a sip from my now-liquified milkshake before responding.

"Sorry, Chad," I smiled, "but with the snowstorm, you know, I think everyone's just going to have to head straight home tonight. But it's so nice to meet you! I'm sure we'll all see each other around."

"Actually, I didn't necessarily mean tonight, *per se*," he stammered. I just smiled and nodded. I know you didn't mean tonight, I willed my friendly eyes to say, but that doesn't change my response: You're not my type. He got the message—smarter than he looked, thank god—and this time we both reddened. I felt like a bitch, but I knew the more I talked, the more awkward it would be.

"Okay, well, hey, I'll let you get back to your reading then. I was just on my way to get some grub and thought I'd say 'hi.'"

"Try a hot dog on a stick. They're hot-diggity delicious, you know," I said, trying to lighten the mood. "Nice meeting you!"

Poor Chad. Plenty of girls would have given their left kidney to date the likes of him, but I wasn't into players trying to score, either figuratively or literally. I wasn't into boys at all, at the moment, thanks to being thoroughly betrayed by Brian. Grrrr.

Luckily, the image of he-who-broke-my-heart-into-a-thousand-pieces wasn't allowed to linger in my mind. No sooner had Chad taken his dejected leave of me than Colin, a waiter at Cheeze Monkey pizzeria, turned up at my table in full clown regalia. God, what was it with this place and the shame-inducing attire?

"Hey, Bozo," I deadpanned, examining Colin's exasperated face.

"Yeah, yeah, Weiner Girl, like I haven't heard that one? I need help, ASAP. I fled Cheeze Monkey because I just can't take it anymore."

"Did someone sock you in the groin with the Whack-a-Mole mallet again?"

"No, ughh. And *please* don't remind me of that."

"Okay, then what?"

"It's dead down there with the snow and all . . . they said we could start closing up once everyone leaves."

"So, that sounds like a good thing."

"Tell that to the one remaining family in the restaurant—some yuppie couple with *seven*—oh yes, you heard me—*SEVEN* kids. Children is too benign a word to describe them. Snot-nosed, pants-pooping, spawns of Satan is more accurate."

"Sorry, Colin, but that's the nature of the beast in your line of work."

"But it's been hours, Miranda! Hours! And they won't leave already! My lungs might actually give out if I have to make them one more stupid balloon animal. It's like *Sesame Street* on a bad acid trip over there, and now they just ordered dessert and plunked down another fifty bucks on tokens for Skee-ball!"

"Sounds like they're having a good time!"

"I'm not so sure judging by the number of temper tantrums I've witnessed, and that doesn't even begin to describe the parents. The dad was actually clipping his fingernails at the table about an hour ago."

"Oh, the humanity!" I said. "Tough break, I guess."

"You're not supposed to say *tough break*," Colin said, pouting.

"Say what?"

"You're supposed to offer me solutions. Magically make my problem go away. Isn't that what you do?"

"Breeders and their maladjusted three-year-olds aren't exactly my specialty. Hell, maladjusted seventeen-year-olds aren't my specialty these days. It sounds like a really annoying family, but they've got to call it quits soon, right? Can't you hold out a little longer?"

"Oh, c'mon Miranda. Throw me a lifeline!"

"Ritalin-laced lollipops?"

"I'm serious!" Colin said with a laugh, but he truly looked like he was about to blow a gasket.

"Okay, okay," I said, grabbing his hand in both of mine to calm him. "Just give me a second to think."

Across the food court, I heard someone sneeze loudly. One of those shower-of-spit beauties that make everyone in the near vicinity run screaming for the nearest anti-bacterial hand gel.

"That might work." I glanced up at Colin.

"What?"

"The sneeze."

"So."

"So, I don't know much about screaming kids, but I do know how to make them disappear."

"Go on. . . ."

"You've got to get sick." Colin eyed me warily.

"You heard me. Just fake sneeze and fake cough and fake almost-die long enough to scare the living crap out of those parents."

"You mean . . ."

"Acting, my friend," I said. "Channel the most raging bout of airborne illness your deranged little mind can muster. But you've got to make it look like something way worse than your garden variety sniffles. I'm talking Ebola virus, dengue fever, TB. . . ."

"Mad cow disease!"

"Well, that's pushing it, but you get my meaning. God, if only you had a surgical mask. That would really seal the deal. Here." I dabbed my milkshake cup to his temple and cheeks, letting the condensation dampen his skin. "That makes you look kind of feverish."

"And you think the mom and dad will pack up the kids and run for cover from the dude hacking up a lung?"

"That's my theory, anyway. You'll have to prove me right."

"Me likey," Colin said with a grin. "In fact, I think I'm beginning to feel a bit of a tickle in the back of my throat." Employing serious dramatic flair, he proceeded to hack and cough and finally hocked up what sounded like an enormous wad of spit.

"You're disgusting."

"And you're a genius," he said, grabbing my hand and kissing it wetly in appreciation. "Germ boy lives! I'll let you know what happens. See you at Ariel's party." He giddily shuffled off in his polka-dot print overalls, and I could hear him practicing his coughs and sneezes as he headed back down toward his end of the mall.

Not surprisingly, my shake no longer seemed appetizing. I instead focused on the novel on my lap for quite a while, but touché, at this point in the book Emma was getting one hell of a verbal smackdown from Mr. Knightly for her inappropriate conduct. "*Rebuke = redemption!*" my mom had scribbled in the margins. Yeah, right. Growing up, it was hard not to wonder if I'd been denied some priceless pearls of advice or wisdom that Mom might have had to offer me were she still alive. But the meaningless insight she'd scribbled here left me convinced I wasn't missing out on much. If she were around to hear it, I'd tell her that I'd been recently rebuked up one side and down the other, and there was not a damn thing redeeming about the experience. Demeaning was more like it. Feeling as though it was hitting just a little too close to home, I dog-eared the page, closed the book, and made my way back toward the Hot-Dog Kabob booth. Ariel would cheer me up.

"*Guess* who came by?" she very nearly wheezed at me when I showed up and lifted the hinged counter separating customer from food service worker.

"Okay, I'll guess, but only once you assure me you're not suffering some kind of massive coronary."

"Chad Mathers!!!!" she squealed. "Hypers!!!!"

"Yeah . . . *and???*"

"*THE* Chad Mathers!"

"Oh, right," I replied, grabbing for my apron and slipping it back over my jumper. "And you're excited about this because. . . ?"

"He asked me if I would double-dip his dog!"

"Ewww. That sounds pornographic."

"What? He likes his corn dogs extra crispy."

"Okay, Ariel. As long as you weren't salivating from the mouth like you are now." Girlfriend clearly had a crush on this Chad Mathers person. She wasn't exactly the sort of chick a guy who looked like Chad would be into, so I opted to change the subject lest I accidentally stoke the flames of her unrequited passion. No sense in getting the girl's hopes up.

"What's the latest on the White Plague?" I asked. "Are we going to blow this Popsicle stand early tonight?" I sort of hoped that wasn't the case, since I had things all worked out with Grady to bring Ariel's birthday cake around at nine.

"Business as usual, from what I can tell. But we should ask Troy. Hey, Troy!" Ariel splayed her belly onto the counter and leaned far over to look into the food stall directly next to us. It was a rotisserie chicken place called Spitfire. Troy Beck's freckled face peeked back from around the corner of the wall.

"Yes, m'lady," he said without batting an eyelash before locking his baby blues on mine. "Oh, hey, Miranda. I was waiting for you to get back. Gotta favor." He slid underneath his counter and popped up in front of ours.

"I already told you how to smooth things over with your girlfriend, Troy," I said. "I can't be your Cyrano twenty-four seven."

"Oh that's all covered. I did exactly as you suggested. Nice call, by the way—Lauren totally forgave me."

"And so you need my help because. . . ." I acted annoyed by these frequent requests from people for advice, but secretly, I relished the attention. Besides, I really was that good at it.

"Here's the thing," Troy said. "Lauren's kid brother is in the hospital. He's got some sort of—"

"Oh that's horrible," Ariel and I said in unison.

"It's okay," Troy said. "He came through surgery and things are looking good. But the thing is . . . I kind of promised Lauren I'd get him a copy of the new snowboarding game, *Avalanche X*." He pantomimed what was apparently supposed to indicate a tricky snowboard maneuver, but looked more like a reenactment of Buster Keaton slipping on a banana peel. "It's the only thing that will cheer him up. The kid's had a rough year."

"Can't you just buy a copy?" Ariel said.

"If you're short on cash, don't expect me to be your loan shark," I said.

"No, it's not that. I *wish*." He shook his head. "Haven't you seen it on TV? The game is sold out all over town. Has been for weeks."

"What makes you think I would be able to get you a copy?" I said, considering his request as I added straws to the dispenser.

"Well, it was worth a try." He sighed and turned back toward the Spitfire counter.

"Wait a sec." I crossed my arms thoughtfully. "Don't give up so easily. It's really for a sick kid?"

"Yeah," he said, looking hopeful. "Can you help?"

"Maybe." Smiling, I began to formulate my latest brilliant plot. Might just be able to kill two birds with one stone. "I'm not promising anything, but. . . ."

"No, I totally understand," Troy nodded his head, his face flushed with appreciation. "That's great, Miranda. Whatever you can do. I totally appreciate it. Better get back to work," he said, waving. "And if this works out, I owe you a solid. Again." I watched as Troy disappeared behind the wall that separated our booths.

"Miranda," Ariel's eyes narrowed as she considered me. "You shouldn't have promised Troy that. He'll get the poor little kid's hopes up." She crossed her arms and looked at me accusingly.

"Ariel, I said I'd *try*. I didn't say I could do it. Besides, I have a plan. And you should be pleased to know it involves your new friend."

"What new friend?"

"The magician, of course."

"Magician?" Ariel looked confused.

"Ariel, *really*. . . ." I rolled my eyes. "CALEB. Jeez. Now, do you want to help me with the plan or just stand around looking confused?"

"Sure, I'll help!" she said. "What should I do first? Reconnaissance?"

"No, let's start with some counter intelligence, as in mind the counter. You hang out here and keep an eye on things while I go have a little chat with Caleb."

"Okay, what should I do if anyone asks where you are?"

"Ariel, do I have to think of everything?" I tossed her my apron with one hand as I lifted up the counter with the other. "I'll be back in ten."

Exiting the food court, I glanced down the corridor and saw in the distance what looked like a herd of Ewoks on the move. Upon closer inspection, I realized it was a family of nine, bundled up like mini Michelin men in hats, scarves, and puffy coats. It could only have been Colin's Cheeze Monkey hellions heading toward the exit. I smiled in satisfaction. I still had the magic touch.

CHAPTER FIVE

Now My Charms Are All O'erthrown

As I rode up the escalator on my way to Got Games, Quinn from Bead Bungalow was on her way down. I was surprised because she typically avoided the bowels of the mall at all costs, though I can't say I blamed her. Her red hair was pulled into a high ponytail and colorful beads draped from her elegant neck. She waved at me, gold bangles jangling. As usual she looked more like a gorgeous gypsy fortune teller than a mall employee. "Miranda," she called out as she passed me. "Have you seen Mike? He's been missing for a few hours and I'm starting to get worried." I remembered Ariel's gossip that Quinn and Mike had recently become an item.

"He wasn't at Treasure Hunt when I passed it on my way in, but I figured he was on his break or in the back room," I said, glancing at my watch. "It's only an hour till closing. Maybe he decided to skip out early on account of the snow. Or maybe one of those psychotic-looking porcelain dolls came to life and strangled him." Quinn's brow furrowed at my joke. Oops. My big mouth and my innate sarcasm got me into trouble more times than I could count, and this was just another example. "Just kidding," I said louder as she reached the bottom of the escalator and I neared the top. "I'm sure it's nothing. I'll ask around and see if anyone's seen him recently."

Still feeling like a heel from my run-in with Quinn, I rounded the corner and came upon the Got Games storefront. A hangout for local multiplayer netheads and board game enthusiasts, Got Games was basically a nerd's paradise. Exhibit A for why this was my first visit. The place screamed "warlock's low-budget bachelor pad," with walls painted floor-to-ceiling black and affixed with cheap star decals. Near the back of the shop, I spied Caleb engaged in conversation with a customer who was hidden from my view at the end of an aisle piled high with classic family board games. As

I sidled up, I realized it wasn't a customer—it was Chad Mathers, apparently still milking his break. As soon as he spotted me, the poor guy blushed from head to toe and stammered something about needing to head back to his post at the Cleat Locker.

"See you tonight, Chad," Caleb said as Ariel's fantasy dreamboat backed away, all but stumbling over his sneakers. Tonight? Caleb was ditching my invite to Ariel's birthday party so that he could hang out with some dumb jock? Talk about your odd couple.

"Sorry to interrupt," I said. "What's happening tonight?"

"Oh, nothing you'd be interested in." Most likely true, I thought, though his cagey response annoyed me a little.

"If it involves the likes of lug nut Chad Mathers, you're probably right," I said.

"Really?" Caleb replied. "I was under the impression that 'lug nuts' were a lucrative market for you." He picked up a price tag gun and began tagging boxes of Magic Eight Balls.

"What's that supposed to mean?" I flushed.

"Your rep precedes you," he said without looking up from his task at hand. "Not that it's my business. I don't judge. Besides, Ariel likes you, so I figure you must be okay."

Embarrassed that a virtual stranger apparently knew the complete *dossier* on my fall from grace at Eastern Prep, I was bordering on speechless. Gossip traveled at warp speed these days, it would seem.

"Did you need something?" he said, getting straight to the point. His brusque self-confidence threw me off my game. I was used to granting people favors—not requesting them. I shifted my weight and scratched my left ankle with the toe of my right sneaker. I wasn't sure how to play this guy.

"Well, I was on my break and I thought I'd come by and say hi." I smiled in my most winning manner. Inveigling 101: Open the door a crack with your charm and then waltz right in.

"Okay," said Caleb, with an elaborate shrug, though I thought I spotted a little blush creeping slowly over his face. That's better. Now I was getting somewhere. Except for the fact that he didn't seem to have much interest in holding up his end of the conversation. God, was this guy socially clueless.

"Also," I said, "I wanted to know if by any chance you could score me a copy of *Avalanche X*." I hadn't meant to just blurt it out like that, but this guy had a way of rattling me.

"*What?*" he said, looking incredulous. "Oh right. I knew you didn't come up here just to chat." He shook his head in disgust. "GAME OVER" flashed in my head. "Even if I could get you that game—an impossibility, by the way—what makes you think I'd go out of my way to hook you up?"

"But it's not for me. . . ." Forget it. It wasn't worth this. Clearly Caleb was a jerk and I wasn't going to lower myself by begging.

"Of course it's not for you. You probably just want to turn around and resell it for a hundred-percent markup, opportunist that you are." Ouch. Now *that* really wasn't fair.

"You know, you're not as smart as you think you are." It was the best comeback I could muster. "Maybe if you actually gave me a chance you'd realize—"

Caleb turned over a Magic Eight Ball and peered into its murky depths.

"Not Likely," he said, holding up the toy to let me see the prediction it offered. "I can put your name on the waiting list with all the other 'regular people.' I know that might be a foreign concept for you, but it's the best I can do."

"No. Forget I asked," I said and turned toward the exit. I was seething. This was a huge mistake.

"Hang on," Caleb called after me. I turned back, thinking he was going to apologize, and waited for him to say something. He looked me straight in the eye long enough that I started to feel a little uncomfortable under his scrutiny. There was something almost mesmerizing about his eyes, which were the color of a stormy sea. "Give this to Ariel, since I can't make it to her party," he finally said, tossing me a rectangular object enclosed in a plastic Got Games bag. I plucked it from the air and turned on my heel, fuming.

I kept my head down as I stepped back onto the escalator, but the sound of nearby giggling made me survey the panoramic view of the ground level below me. The Itneys were exiting the Luxe Labels boutique like a couple of jackals emerging from their cave, laden with shopping bags. On a bench in front of the store, Rachel was sitting on Brian's lap, stroking his hair and peppering his forehead with kisses. Once the Itneys interrupted their love-fest, the foursome took off in the direction of the movie theaters. I felt like throwing up.

"Success?" Ariel wondered when I returned to Hot-Dog Kabob, eyeing the white cellophane bag from Caleb. I shook my head dejectedly.

"No," I said, hastily stashing her present near my purse under the counter. Ariel's neck craned to where I'd hidden the gift behind a roll of paper towels and she looked at me suspiciously for a moment before her eyes registered a new thought.

"Oh. Oh! By the way, Riley and Brooke came by looking for you a few minutes ago."

"Who?"

"Riley and Brooke. From the Dress Depot."

"What did they want?"

"They're feuding over what music to play in the store. Riley wants death metal, but Brooke insists on hip-hop. They want you to arbitrate. I told them you'd call over there when you got back. Do you want the number?"

"Let them figure it out on their own. Why does everyone insist on making their problems mine, anyway? I'm freaking sick of it!"

Ariel jumped as I slammed my palm down on the counter in frustration. I immediately regretted letting Caleb, Brian, Rachel, and the Itneys turn me into such a Debbie Downer, especially when Ariel's surprise party was less than an hour away. I hoped Grady didn't forget his promise to fetch her ice cream cake from Just Desserts later.

"Oh, hey, you haven't seen Mike pass by here while I was gone, have you?" I asked Ariel, attempting to shift my mood to a more pleasant one. "Quinn says he's MIA."

"Yeah, she came by here and asked me, too. I haven't seen him."

"I bet he took off early."

"But without locking down the store?" Ariel said with a frown. "That's not like him."

"Speaking of," I changed the subject. "Let's start packing up this joint. No way are we going to get any more customers before nine."

"I'll grab the mop," Ariel said.

CHAPTER SIX

These Are Not Natural Events

"You called Chad a LUG NUT?" Ariel stared at me, mouth agape as if I'd just picked a bar fight with the Dalai Lama.

"Not to his face!" I sighed, needlessly organizing the stack of red-and-white-checkered cardboard boats we served the corn dogs in.

"Do you even *know* what he scored on his SATs?"

"Like I'm supposed to know this?"

"Miranda, he's a cerebral phenom. Marshall High made it to nationals in the Academic Decathlon last year thanks to him."

"Are we talking about the same Chad Mathers? The guy whose neck is thicker than your waist?"

"Total brainiac."

"But he's a *football* player!"

"Slash brainiac." Ariel was shaking her head now, like I had somehow failed to properly kneel before the pope. "Slash *dreamy*. . . ." my coworker added in a near whisper.

For a girl who was homeschooled, Ariel certainly managed to know a lot about our fellow mall employees. If what she was saying about Chad was true, I couldn't help but feel more than a little discomfited at having summarily dismissed him as having all brawn and no brain. It was making more sense now why he and Caleb seemed to be tight. They both went to the same school and perhaps weren't at opposing ends of the mental spectrum after all, though they certainly didn't look like they ran in the same circles. I wondered if it was too late to track Chad down and see if he'd attend my little soiree for Ariel, which would be the equivalent of inviting the latest babyfaced boy band to a preteen-packed bat mitzvah. Maybe he could just swing by on his way out after work. I needed an excuse to vamoose so that I could drop by the Cleat

Locker and ask him. I only hoped he wouldn't think I was asking him to come because I was interested in him!

"I think I'm going to go check on Riley and Brooke after all," I told Ariel, throwing a disgusting gray washcloth back in the bucket of disgusting gray water. "You know, make sure they didn't claw each other's eyes out." Ariel's face registered skepticism and she crossed her arms decidedly.

"You're up to something," she said.

"Say what?"

"You've been acting weird all night."

"Whatever. *Unicorn Fantasy* is affecting your brain."

"No." She shook her head. "Ever since those friends from your school—the ones with too much makeup and that pretty boy—came by here, you've been a little whack-a-doo."

"They're not my friends."

I wish she hadn't reminded me. The Cleat Locker was on the ground floor near the movie theaters, in the same direction I'd just seen my ex-boyfriend and his harem heading. I'd ditched my hot dog hat, but that didn't make me feel any more confident about possibly running into my social detractors yet again tonight. Still, it would be worth it if I could convince Chad to come to Ariel's birthday party. And who couldn't I convince of almost anything, crotchety Caleb notwithstanding?

I continued to ruminate on the grumpy gamemaster's rudeness as I ambled in the direction of Siberia, past the tchotchke-filled greeting card store and the Blissworks Body Shop, when slam!— rent-a-cop Grady came barreling around the corner by Rockin' Tots children's boutique completely out of breath and seemingly alarmed.

"Whoa, Five-O!" I grabbed him by the shoulders to steady myself since he'd nearly knocked me off my feet. "Where's the fire?"

"Miranda, hey," he said. "So sorry—can't talk now." He brushed past me, guns-a-blazing, metaphorically speaking. Can't talk now? Since when did Grady *not* have time for *moi*?

"Don't forget about the cake!" I called after him, wondering if there was any reason for his mad dash beyond his own propensity to act like a member of the vice squad. Feeling less-than-confident that Ariel's birthday cake from the other side of the mall would make its way to the food court by nine, I hurried on to the Cleat Locker. "Mensa" Mathers was pulling down the metal grate in preparation for closing, but I scuttled underneath in a half-limbo maneuver.

"Not so fast . . . you've still got twenty minutes on the clock," I said, trying to temper my charm to appear as platonic as possible. He blushed for the twelfth time tonight.

"Slow night," he said, grinning sheepishly and leaving the grate halfway up. "If you're looking for snow boots, by the way, you'll have to try Celebrity Footwear. We only sell athletic shoes."

"I'm not here to shop." I followed him back to the cash register where he had a small TV behind the counter tuned to local news.

"They're predicting four feet by morning," he said, leaning his elbows on the counter to watch the footage. A live camera shot panned across a lamp-lit street that was abandoned except for a few stray cars which had skidded off the road. An on-scene reporter in a pink puffy jacket, Moscovian fur hat, and giant ski gloves looked as though this wasn't her most plumb assignment to date. Her eyes were watery and her nose looked like a maraschino cherry, but to her credit, her freezing schnoz matched her lips, which were perfectly lipstick-lined.

"It's really rough out there," Chad said. "The mayor just issued a citywide curfew to keep drivers off the road."

"What? How are we supposed to get home?"

"If you don't have your own personal snow plow or a really good four-wheel drive, good luck."

Like all football players, I assumed Chad was merely resorting to a manly sense of hyperbole, so I ignored him as well as my creeping doubts about trying to navigate my car home through what was shaping up to be a full-on blizzard. Surely it couldn't have gotten *that* bad in the four hours since I'd arrived at work. I was about to launch into my invitation to Ariel's birthday bash when we heard the screeching sound of a whistle. Seconds later, another referee-shirted beefcake swung his way under the half-open storefront grate. Chad's coworker, I presumed. He dropped the whistle from between his lips.

"Dude, come quick," he said, panting as he beckoned Chad into the mall's thoroughfare. "Somebody just went all Butch Cassidy on the computer store! Shit is going DOWN out here!"

Chad hurried off with his coworker, leaving me to follow. Instead, I picked up the phone at the register to dial mall security, but the line was dead. Crap, the snow must have downed a phone line. A robbery?! Jeez, there were plenty of crimes of fashion around this joint, but in terms of real misconduct, minor graffiti and parking infractions were the worst offenses Grady ever had to deal with. No wonder he was burning rubber a few minutes ago when I literally ran into him. He must have just heard about the robbery . . . or was he chasing down the perps? In any case, my ice cream cake errand boy clearly had more pressing business. I'd have to hurry to the other side of the mall to pick it up before Just Desserts closed for the night. But first, I wanted to see what the commotion was all about. I stooped back under the gate of the Cleat Locker and turned left down the mall's main drag. Two hundred yards away in front of PC Pro, a crowd of mall employees had already gathered.

"What happened?" I asked breathlessly once I'd woven my way over to Chad and his equally brawny (though shorter) coworker, whose nametag identified him as "Dex." Standing head-and-shoulders above the crowd, Chad answered absentmindedly as his eyes scanned the surroundings, seemingly looking for someone or something.

"Someone ripped off the place. They got away with a couple of laptops, a bunch of tablets, and pretty much all the MP3 players. Smashed the display cases to get to them."

My palm instinctively went to my mouth.

"Was anyone hurt?" I asked.

"No one was there," Dex said. "Luckily the manager had locked up early and sent the employees home before the roads got impassable."

"The gate was down, then." I tried to piece together the details. "So whoever did it got in through the back corridor?"

"It would seem that way; no one else working down here saw anything amiss."

I felt a tap on my shoulder and swiveled around to see Colin, still wearing his clown getup.

"Word travels fast," he said, inching forward in the crowd of onlookers to try and get a better look. "Who do they think did it?"

"You got me," I said, displaying my palms.

"Where's that dweeby security guard, anyway? Didn't anybody call the cops?"

"On a night like tonight, I'm sure the police force is spread pretty thin," Dex said.

"And the landlines might be out," I said. "I couldn't get a dial tone on the phone just now."

I craned my neck to see into the computer store. Display shelves were broken and scattered about the floor, apparently toppled by the criminal in his haste. It occurred to me that Grady had his work cut out for him—though he'd probably relish his moment playing in the security world's equivalent of the "big leagues" for a change.

"Only a moron would try to make a break for it with the weather what it is right now," said Chad's coworker, "but whoever it was, it looks like he means business."

"If we're locked in, that means the thief is stuck here, too," Colin pointed out.

"What do you mean 'locked in?'" I asked.

"You haven't heard?"

"Heard what?" Dex, Chad, and I asked simultaneously.

"The citywide curfew. We're not allowed to leave. Grady stopped by Cheeze Monkey about an hour ago and told us the mall was in lockdown until morning. Direct orders from the bigwigs at corporate. They're afraid they'll get sued if someone runs their car off the road leaving work, so we've got to wait till the snowplows make their initial rounds."

"But how long will that take?" Chad said, glancing at his watch in dismay.

"Sunrise, if we're lucky. Dude," Dex elbowed Chad, "so much for your big night. Looks like you just got upstaged by a snowstorm."

"I've got to go call Caleb," Chad said. "He's going to blow a gasket."

"But they can't just keep us here against our will!" I turned back to Colin, starting to fume.

"True in theory. You could sweet-talk Grady into unlocking the doors for you, I suppose. But your car is buried past its tires in snow right now. You want to try walking home? Because that's suicide by snowbank."

"So we're *literally* marooned here for the night? With some shoplifter on steroids?" I sighed. "I'd better get back and let Ariel and the gang know what's up." My tone may have suggested concern for my defenseless coworkers, but in reality, I was semi-thrilled at the opportunity to relate the dramatic turn of events to a captive audience. I took off for the food court.

CHAPTER SEVEN

Come, Temperate Nymphs, and Help to Celebrate

"But I'm sure if the burglar is even the least bit competent, he'll have had more than one exit strategy," I said to Alfredo, who had joined us from upstairs and was listening to my update along with my fellow food courtesans. "He's probably long gone by now." I hoped I sounded a lot more confident than I felt.

Ariel looked unconvinced, so I changed the subject. "Since we're trapped in this hell hole for the night, we might as well have some fun." I stood up from my chair and clapped my hands. "Troy, you're in charge of music. Turn off this Muzak crap and put on something we can dance to. And make it loud," I called after him as he rushed off. Ignoring Ariel's worried frown, I steered her back toward the Hot-Dog Kabob booth and shot a look at Alfredo to usher her the rest of the way.

"What's going on?" my coworker said, unaware that she was about to get one of Alfredo's Five-Minute Makeover treatments.

"I promise it won't hurt," Alfredo said. "Well, not unless tweezers are required."

With Ariel out of earshot, I turned to Fro-Yo's Derek, who looked at me expectantly.

"Take the Sloth Rocket," I said, using our name for the vehicle that the decrepit janitorial director Simpson used to get from one end of the mall to the other. "Head over to Just Desserts, pick up Ariel's cake, and get back here as quickly as you can." I glanced at the clock adding, "Our guests should be arriving any minute now, and Alfredo can't keep Ariel occupied for too long."

I was standing on a chair hanging "streamers," a.k.a. spools of receipt paper, from pillar to pillar when Caleb and Chad showed up. Funny those two being friends. Ballhead and the Beast.

"Chad! Glad you could make it!" I smiled, figuring he might be the best present I could give Ariel. "And if it isn't Mr. Got Games himself . . . I thought you were too *coool* for our little party."

"I never said that," Caleb said, with a moody glare. "Figured since we're stuck here for the night, I might as well come."

"I'm sure Ariel will appreciate the colossal sacrifice."

Chad shuffled from one foot to the other, eying Caleb and me uncomfortably. I'm sure he wondered at the obvious friction, but I figured I'd let Caleb enlighten him.

Just then Grady came galumphing into the food court, practically hyperventilating. He paused to catch his breath, coming precariously close to smashing the pink ice cream cake box gripped in his hands.

"Sorry I'm late!" he said, gasping for air. "Dinah was still frosting the cake when I got there. I made it over here as quick as I could."

I glanced at my watch—it was 9:08.

"Grady! Jeez, I hardly expected you to pick up the cake with everything else you've had to deal with tonight!" The guard stared at me confused. "Hello? The lockdown? The wayward computer thief?"

"Oh right," Grady said. "Well, no need to worry yourself about all that."

"You mean you caught the guy?" Chad asked. Clearly still winded from his sprint across the mall with a ten-pound cake, Grady looked flustered.

"Afraid I can't speak to an investigation that's still pending," he said. "But I didn't want to let you and Ariel down, Miranda." He nodded toward the cake which, as I removed the plastic cover, I could see didn't survive the trip fully intact. The icing was smeared and the melting ice cream underneath was starting to leak onto the tray.

"Looks like it says 'Happy Birthday, Awol,'" Caleb said. I shot him a dirty look. Could this dude be any more pessimistic?

"Ariel will be too excited to even notice the difference," I said. "Grady, did I ever tell you you're my hero? Thanks so much! Too bad you probably can't stick around for the party, with all the chaos around here. . . ."

Grady's face, at first beaming from my praise, flashed to disappointment.

"Thanks for the offer, Miranda, but not when I'm on duty." I heard someone behind me just about snort with laughter. Grady's police playacting was admittedly ridiculous, but part of me felt a little sorry for him. I got the sense that he was just a very lonely man trying to feel important in the world. Sadly, I could relate. He was about to head back out into the mall when I called him back.

"If you have time later, feel free to come back down and have some cake. By the way, you don't think we're in any danger, right? I mean, with the burglary and all?"

"Don't worry, Miranda. If the perp's still onsite, they'll have to deal with me." Somehow, this didn't have the comforting effect I'm sure he intended. "In the meantime—"

"Hey, Grady," Troy said, "why don't you deputize us? We can help you go *Die Hard* on the dude." He and a few of the guys whistled and gave each other high-fives.

"Listen, this isn't a joke," Grady said, terse warning in his voice. "I'm going to issue a strong proviso that you all stick together and stay in the food court. The last thing I need is a bunch of rogue mall employees interfering with a criminal investigation."

Troy gave a comically demonstrative military salute as Grady stomped off. When he was out of earshot, Caleb turned to Troy and said, "*Die Hard*, huh? With what, your bare hands, hotshot?"

As the guys tried to one-up one another with a lame display of martial arts moves, I bustled around putting the finishing touches on the surprise party. With the pressure on to save Ariel's birthday from a night of abysmal boredom, a half-melted cake and some flimsy decorations just weren't going to cut it. I'd have to come up with something bigger and better to distract her if we were going to survive the lockdown. Apparently Chad and I were on the same wavelength. As I retrieved a box of candles from my pocket, he sidled over.

"So, Miss Cruise Director, given any thought to what we're going to do after this? It's pretty clear even to me, a quote unquote 'lug nut'—"

"How did you. . . ? Caleb told you!" I started to turn toward Caleb to bawl him out, but Chad stopped me. My face flushed with embarrassment, an emotion I was getting more and more acquainted with in recent days. "Well, now I feel stupid."

"Hey, it's no big deal," he said with a chuckle. "No hard feelings." He held out his hand to shake mine. "Just don't be so quick to judge the next guy. Anyway," he said, "I was thinking that if we're going to be in here all night. . . ." he trailed off as he gazed at something over my shoulder. I turned around to see Alfredo, leading a reluctant Ariel by the hand.

"*Voila!*" he said as he whirled her in front of him with a dramatic flourish. Admittedly, even I was surprised at how great she looked. She'd always been cute in a Keebler Elf kind of way, but now her best features really stood out. Her kinky hair was pinned up with just a few rivulets caressing her face. Light pink lip gloss and some subtle glitter shadow around her eyes—boy, Alfredo really knew his subject—completed Ariel's transformation. She went from looking like my surrogate kid sister to becoming one of those ethereal fairies from *The Lord of the Rings*. If Chad's face was pink, Ariel's was red and getting redder by the second. Thankfully, just as it was clear that she was about to bolt back into the kitchen in embarrassment at all the fuss, someone started singing "Happy Birthday" and we all joined in.

"Blow out the candles," I said to Ariel. "And don't forget to make a wish."

"Okay, I wish—"

"Don't *tell* us!"

"Let me guess," a cutting voice said from behind my shoulder. "She wishes she had a chance in hell of ever getting laid in her lifetime." Ariel's pink cheeks paled. What the . . ?! I swiveled on my heel and put a face to the voice I already recognized.

"I don't remember inviting you, Brian," I said, steam practically escaping my ears. I nodded toward the Itneys, who stood behind Rachel looking smugly satisfied with arms crossed. Britney blew a bubble with her wad of chewing gum and let it smack loudly. "That goes double for your hangers-on," I continued. "And, really, for a guy so incredibly vocal about what an insult I am to humanity, you have an uncanny way of pseudo-stalking me. Now, please leave. *All* of you."

"Gladly," Rachel answered for the group, tossing her tacky blonde extensions over one shoulder in defiance. "We're not interested in your little charity case's birthday party, I can assure you. But since our shopping excursion morphed into getting stuck here for the night, we just thought we'd come see what all the bottom-feeders were up to."

There was silence as the food courtesans all waited for me to respond. Once again, I felt my eyes sting and willed them not to pool up with tears. Wracking my brain for some clever retort, I found I was too enraged to speak. It was one thing for them to pick on me. I deserved it in some messed-up way. But Ariel and the rest of the geeks who worked down here were innocent and undeserving of their cruel scorn. How was it possible that I was ever friends with these arrogant SOBs? I shuddered, remembering the similar crown of condescension I wore back when I stood perched on a higher rung of the social stratum. Looking at the Itneys with their matching boots and Rachel with her pricey leather satchel—all three with scowls on their faces—was like having a mirror held up in front of me. Had I been such a bitch like them? Was I still? While these thoughts raced through my brain, the unlikeliest of allies entered the fray to give me a reprieve.

"Why are you guys down here, anyway?" Caleb said. "Didn't you hear that the Highway Patrol is sending a helicopter to the south parking lot to start taking people out of here in small groups? You're going to be at the back of the queue if you don't get over there."

Whitney's eyes lit up, but then she eyed Caleb suspiciously, apparently on to his whopper of a lie.

"So why aren't you guys heading over there?"

"What, you think any of us have anything better to do on a Saturday night? This is the most excitement we've had in years! We're staying put. But you'd better hurry. I heard they're only making a limited number of chopper runs for people who can plead emergency cases."

"Really?" Britney said.

"Where do you think all your other classmates are right now? They've probably already called dibs."

"Maybe we can still make the ski trip tomorrow!" Britney turned to Rachel and Brian excitedly. The other three still looked skeptical, but the look on Brian's face meant he wasn't about to call Caleb's bluff if there really might be a chance to get out of here.

"Ladies, let's leave the plebes to their lame little party," he said. As they headed in the direction of the mall's south exit, the snickers and scoffs of Brian, Rachel, and the Itneys echoed through the food court.

"That's it," I said. "I'm not going to take this anymore."

"They're gone now. It's over; let's just enjoy the party," Caleb said.

"This may just seem like a tempest in a teapot to you, but it's about a lot more than the party—even though I did spend all day planning this." I gritted my teeth. "That's beside the point. They can mess with me, but I will absolutely not allow them to mess with Ariel."

"Do you really mean that?" Ariel asked. Her eyes lit up, briefly, but I could tell from her face that she was still feeling stung by Rachel's comments.

"Of course, Ariel," I said, not quite realizing till this moment how much I cared about her. "And don't you worry. We've got all night to make them pay. But for right now, let's just enjoy your party. You only turn seventeen once, after all!"

Ariel was back to her chipper self an hour later after opening a slew of presents, including a travel chess set from Caleb.

"This is my kind of game," he said. "Keep it around for when you get bored with video games—and, believe me, you will. Chess challenges you like nothing else. Kings and queens have been playing it for centuries."

While she was oohing and ahhing over her haul, Caleb sidled up to me.

"Thanks," I said, blushing.

"For what?"

"Getting rid of those jerks earlier. They almost ruined Ariel's night, but we showed them. . . ."

"Whoa, whoa, easy with the 'we' stuff. I don't know those guys and I don't care to know them. Whatever your beef is with them, and vice versa, just leave me out of it."

I didn't understand his sudden gruffness. Hadn't he seen the way Rachel had just slammed Ariel? Hadn't he come to her rescue? Why was he being so hostile again?

Before I could argue my point further, Derek from Fro-Yo-Yo and Colin, his clown makeup smeared with perspiration, came running into the food court.

"They've taken over Worthington's Drug Store, Teasers, and Camperville," Derek said, gasping for breath. "They won't let anyone in."

"They said that it's first come, first served," Colin said.

"No, they said finders keepers."

"*Whatever.* They took over the department store with all the best stuff in it and the one store that had sleeping bags and survival gear!" Derek said, nearly shouting.

"Who's 'they?'" I asked suspiciously.

"A bunch of the Eastern Prep kids, including that a-hole, Brian, who was in here before, and his girlfriend. For the record, they're majorly P.O.d about the whole 'helicopter' story."

"Who cares what they're doing as long as they're at the other end of the mall?" Ariel seemed unperturbed. "We're just in here for the night. What do we need with all that stuff, anyway?"

"Don't you get it?" Derek answered. "We don't know what's happening out there with the storm. We could be snowed in here for days. What if we lose power? This could turn into a survival game."

"See?" I said to Caleb chidingly. "It's war. You're involved now whether you want to be or not."

"Wait a sec," Chad said, "before we get ahead of ourselves. . . . Don't we have bigger things to worry about? Like, oh, I don't know . . . the computer store thief?"

"What about him?" I said with a shrug.

"Well, he's *probably* not still here, but what if he strikes again?"

"Citizen's arrest," Troy said, pulling a pair of handcuffs out of his back pocket.

"Where did you get those?" I asked, rolling my eyes.

"On eBay."

"They aren't even real," Caleb said. "We sell some just like those at Got Games."

"Oh, they're real," Troy said.

"Let me try them out," I said in a wheedling tone. Troy snapped one of the heavier-than-expected cuffs around my wrist and I jangled it in the air. "They feel real."

"If they're so real, how come I know the trick to get out of them?" Caleb said.

He was starting to annoy me so I grabbed his arm and slapped the other cuff around it.

"Fine, if it's so easy, do it," I said, goading him. "Show us your stupid little magic trick."

He twisted his wrist a few times even though it was clear there was no way he'd be able to get his arm out of them. He looked confused. I yanked back on my end of the handcuff.

"This is ridiculous," he said. "Just give me the key, Troy."

Troy stuck his hand in his back pocket, then his front pockets.

"This isn't funny," Caleb said. "Unlock us."

"I . . . what the hell? . . . I can't find the key. It was in my pocket," he said. Caleb and I both looked at him expectantly, our irritation growing. "I'm *serious*."

He looked around the ground at his feet and everyone else did, too, but the key was nowhere to be found. Just brilliant. Brian, Rachel, and the Itneys were going all *Lord of the Flies* on us, a potentially armed criminal might or might not be somewhere in the mall, and Caleb and I were handcuffed together. What more could go wrong?

CHAPTER EIGHT

All Men Idle, All. And Women Too

The last of Ariel's birthday cake was now a soupy mess, in contrast to the thigh-high-and-growing snowdrifts deposited by the blizzard outside. Sprawled lazily among and atop the tables in the food court, close to two-dozen partycrashers intermingled with our original band of misfits. An apparently intense game of paper football was well underway near the unsuitably formal Baccarat crystal chandelier that hovered over the entrance to the food court, while another congregation of gearheads had accessed the CO_2 tanks from a soda fountain. "There's a pressure-relief valve on that, you dork. No *way* are you going to be able to make a cannon." A group of girls braided each other's hair while sitting cross-legged in a circle on the floor, Alfredo critically monitoring them like a drill sergeant with a class of new recruits. I surveyed the scene impatiently from my perch atop the counter.

"Do you think Randall will pay us overtime for this?" I said, still being jostled occasionally by my cumbersome Siamese twin. He hadn't stopped scrutinizing the terrazzo tile floor for the nonexistent key. "Dude, you're yanking my arm from its socket. Give it a rest, already. We've looked everywhere."

Caleb exhaled loudly, ran his free hand through his thick mane of hair, and brought his surly stare eye level with mine.

"This blows," he said, removing a bottle of water from my grasp. "And you'd better ease up, because seeing the inside of a ladies' room is not on my bucket list. Not today. Not ever." That particular complication of our conjoinedness had yet to cross my mind. Oh dear. I screwed the plastic cap back on, firmly.

Dex reached for the cell phone from the backside of his too-tight Cleat Locker shorts.

"Maybe I can find out the status on the weather. They've got to be making some sort of headway with the plows."

Lurching past in stops and starts while trying to balance a red plastic tray vertically on his index finger, Troy paused in front of us and brought the tray under his arm like a gym coach with a clipboard.

"Yo, Einstein, we lost cell reception about two hours ago. Why else do you think we're all sitting here bored shitless? The ability for anyone in our generation to self-amuse has sadly been bred out of our species. I blame Bill Gates. What I wouldn't give for a lame game of Words with Friends right about now." He paused and eyed Caleb. "On the other hand . . . you've got a store full of video games up there. With the whole night in front of me I may just have to answer the '*Call of Duty*.'"

"Huh?" I wondered aloud.

"Gamer pun," Ariel translated, chewing on the straw from her cup of Sprite.

Chad broke long enough from doing wall pushups nearby to chime in.

"Come to think of it, I wouldn't mind a little *Rock Band* action. You in, Caleb?"

"Not with *this* ball and chain," he said, nodding in my direction. "Jimi Hendrix never had a sidekick."

Brooke and Riley from the Dress Depot were sitting astride a nearby table, listlessly dipping fries into a paper cup filled with ranch dressing.

"Of all the things you could do in the mall tonight, you want to play stupid video games?" Riley said. "If I had the run of this place, I'd head straight down to Luxe Labels and try on everything in my size. Maybe raid the cosmetics counter, too."

I privately imagined this was exactly what Rachel and the Itneys were currently up to, and then I remembered the larger brigade of my private school classmates, shoppers and mall employees alike, holding dominion on the far side of the building. "Well, we kind of *do* have the run of this place," I said. "But first things first. We need to try to claim some necessities from 'enemy territory' for tonight. They've called dibs on Worthington's and Camperville, which means they're not giving up sleeping bags or toiletries without a fight."

"Surely they can spare some toothpaste," said a tatted-out girl I thought I recognized from Wacko, a.k.a. the emo emporium, located on the mall's upper level.

"Don't bet on it. You guys don't know these people like I know them. But if we're going to be stuck here all night, we shouldn't have to be miserable. I say we send some scouts out to see what kind of supplies we can get."

"I was a Scout! I can do it!" Ariel said, her face beaming. "Sold the most cookies in the tri-state region four years running." I pretended to ignore this not-surprising revelation and the fact that it qualified her for absolutely nothing.

"Troy, you go back out, and take Colin and Derek with you. Grab whatever you think we can use for tonight. Definitely hit up Infinity Homewares for pillows and blankets. Try to score some batteries and flashlights, and maybe a radio, in case the power goes out." I was fairly certain the mall had a backup generator, but figured it was better to err on the side of caution. "The natives are getting restless," I said, scanning the rest of the food court. "The theater will probably keep flicks running all night, but swing by Binder's Books on your way back and bring us an assortment of trashy novels and magazines to help pass the time."

Ariel cupped her hand over my ear and whispered in it. I nodded. "The birthday girl is requesting a run to the bulk candy store. Pixie sticks, if you will. And Red Vines for me . . . oh, on second thought, just bring a random assortment for everyone."

Quinn had approached now, swinging one of her long bead necklaces in circles from her wrist.

"If you're going out, can you keep your eyes peeled for Mike? It's like he vanished into thin air or something." She turned her attention on me. "You do know Grady's not going to like this little Lewis and Clark expedition, right? He told us to stay here."

"You do realize that badge is plastic, right?" I said. "In any case, he is putty in my hands. If Grady's the deputy around here, I'm the sheriff."

"Let the looting and rioting begin," cheered Derek.

"Hold the phone. Those middle-aged ladies at Infinity Homewares scare the crap out of me," Colin confessed with alarmed clown eyes. "I don't think they're just going to let us have stuff for free."

I reflected on the conundrum. Would commandeering a few items on a night like tonight be considered stealing? Certainly not on the same level as stealing computers, right? I couldn't afford to get into anymore trouble. Yet my classmates bivouacking on the other side of the mall seemed to be helping themselves. So why the hell not? Being stuck for who knows how long without any basic creature comforts was going to be miserable. It was a tough call to have to make, but I needed to let my comrades know they could count on me to see them through this whole ordeal.

"You don't have to tear through stores like rabid apes," said Caleb. He'd been standing by my side silently until this moment. I reddened, feeling like one of those Oscar winners who gets hastily ushered off-stage before they can complete their thank-yous. "The other employees shouldn't balk," he said. "It's a state of emergency, and besides, they'll need to eat. Tell 'em they can come down here for free food. We'll help each other out. 'Special circumstances,' after all. Just keep your eyes peeled and be swift about it. We still don't know what's up with whoever ripped off the PC Pro store."

I glanced at the larger group now clustered around us. Everyone seemed to be on the verge of hero worship for Caleb, as if he had just delivered the St. Crispin's Day speech accompanied by a poignantly heart-pounding John Williams score. *". . . Be swift about it . . ."* Who talks that way?

When people began to disperse again, I turned to Caleb in a huff.

"What are you doing, offering free food to the whole mall? What if we run out and don't have enough for ourselves?"

"It's a snowstorm, not Armageddon."

"But if everyone comes down here to score free soft pretzels, it's going to be chaos. I don't want to be overrun by outsiders."

"Oh, I see. Maybe you're better off sticking with 'your own kind.'" He used finger quotes with his free hand, which pissed me off even more. "I'm sure all your Eastern Prep classmates are fine-dining it on fried onion bouquets at Teasers right about now. Maybe you should go join them. Oh . . . but wait." He lifted up his arm, dragging mine with it. "That'd mean you'd have to take me along with you, and having *them* see *you* with *me* on your arm would kill you, wouldn't it? Shit. I meant to tell the guys to find us something that could saw through these before they took off. Maybe Grady can justify his paycheck for once and jimmy these open. We should go look for him."

I was too miffed by Caleb's personal remark to heed his suggestion.

"Let's get a few things straight. For starters, I am not friends with those entitled brats. . . ."

"Oh, that's right. You only date one of them."

"Date-*ed*. Note the past tense."

"Seems like he dumped you, not the other way around."

Technically, there had never been an official breakup. There didn't need to be one after all was said and done. I knew things were over between Brian and me when he stood in the school superintendent's office with his parents and my dad and accused me of being behind the tutoring service that had run amok. It was the truth, to a point. I had conceived of the enterprise as an entirely legit symbiotic relationship between cool kid and whiz kid. But those most in need of academic help typically had too big an ego to publicly own it, and in a growing number of instances, the geeks preferred a currency other than cold hard cash; namely, an entrée (if only brief) to the higher stratosphere of Eastern Prep's cool cliques. An exchange of this sort required the utmost discretion. So I ran things on the down-low, a sort of "black market" operation intended to be win-win for everyone. I'll acknowledge that over time my suspicions were aroused when bobble-headed cheerleaders started making the honor roll and turning up at school dances with skinny "Where's Waldo?" types. The doormats who used to come to school wearing "My Other Car Is a Tardis" T-shirts started rolling into school acting like big ballers. Wads of cash being furtively exchanged around the lockers seemed to be more on par with drug deals than with extra help in calculus. Of course it occurred to me that more than just tutoring must be at play, but perhaps, subconsciously, I didn't want to know. Once I'd gotten my thirty-percent commission for making initial introductions to the study buddies, I didn't concern myself with the particulars. Only when Brian ratted me out as "the ringleader" of the schoolwide scam did I learn the sobering details. Turns out the dunces had started recruiting the brainiacs to take their SATs for them, providing them with fake IDs so that they could easily pass unnoticed at College Board testing sites, where scrutiny was lax at best. Of the eight Eastern Prep students who were eventually caught, one faced felony charges of scheming to defraud (that would be my ex), while the rest faced lesser charges of falsifying business records and criminal impersonation. High-priced attorneys got Brian's butt off the hook by arranging a deal in which he informed on the "real" mastermind behind the scheme, a.k.a. yours truly. I had my Joan of Arc moment in the district attorney's office, but they were unable to prove that I had knowledge of the serious scams—because, god's honest truth, I didn't! (And I'm not sure even my dad believes me on this one.) Since both popular kids and the geeky plebes were wrapped up in the wrongdoing, I was immediately ostracized by virtually every clique at my school and was a natural scapegoat for the school board to throw the book at. My part in the tutoring brokerage firm didn't necessarily amount to criminal, but the fact that I'd profited from it made me guilty in their eyes. Being forced to pay back the money I'd earned from the enterprise (to be ultimately deposited in a scholarship fund) sucked, but Brian's lies were what really hurt. So, too, had my best friend's betrayal.

During the two years we'd been dating, I'd adopted Brian's group of friends as my own, and that had included self-proclaimed "complete fox" Rachel Alonso, whose confidence and general sense of superiority kept pace with my own. When Brian and I first hooked up, she had been dating a senior hottie named Max who ran in the same crowd. Our mutual respect for each other's ability to manipulate and control people using only the words that came out of our mouths led to a fast friendship, and we spent countless nights cackling our asses off at our own little inside jokes, often made at the expense of others. I know, I know . . . classic mean girls. And that's the saddest part of my whole undoing: not being ousted from their social sphere, but being forced to reflect on what a bitch I'd kind of been before all this happened.

Rachel had been single—a status she decried as wholly unnatural—ever since Max abandoned her for college last year. But mere days after the the SAT scam broke open, my former best friend started cozying up to my ex. They wantonly kissed each other at school, their gaping mouths reminding me of those sucker fish that clean algae off aquarium glass. Whatever, they deserve each other, I continued to tell myself. But despite my outward show of pluck and fortitude, I felt injured in the worst way. Not only had Rachel backed up Brian's character assassination of me, telling everyone at school I had cooked up the SAT switcheroo to set Brian up, but she'd also made a mockery of our entire friendship when it became clear she had eyes on my man the whole time. And so I found myself with virtually no friends or sympathizers to speak of, trying to eke out the rest of the school year with at least a feigned degree of dignity. Let me just tell you this: anyone who says leprosy is a disease that's been eradicated hasn't set foot in a high school lately.

After Caleb's last rude remark I'd been giving him the silent treatment, which somehow seemed less effectual and harder to maintain with him chained to my side. When Ariel sidled up next to us a few minutes later, I welcomed the distraction but ended up only getting more heat. Though, to be precise, Ariel usually didn't get pissed so much as mopey and dejected.

"I could have gone with Troy and the guys, you know."

"It wasn't necessary."

"But I could have helped!" she said with a whine. "You act just like my mom sometimes. She keeps me under house arrest and you keep me trapped behind this counter like I'm your slave or something."

"I'm your first-class ticket to fun, and you know it."

"Yeah, but you're always minimizing me. I know you think you have a way with people, or whatever, but I'm no slouch myself."

"So what are you suggesting, Ariel?" I sighed in annoyance and glanced testily at Caleb, who in turn glanced at the ceiling with wide eyes in a mocking "Don't mind me!" face.

Ariel leaned closer to me, once again an overeager puppy.

"Those mean kids," she said. "Why don't you let *me* take a crack at them the next time they come around the food court?"

I had to hide a chuckle trying to imagine Ariel doing anything that could possibly pierce the armor of my friends-turned-foes. Her quirky disposition would irritate them the way a fruit fly might cause you to bat your hand in the air, but she was hardly a match for the likes of them. Or was she? Ariel seemed as harmless and timorous as a fawn, which would make her the perfect decoy for the plot that was now crystallizing in my brain. I knew my coworker had the prowess, tenacity, and—most of all—loyalty to pull it off.

"Well. . . ." I said with a protracted pause. "You really think you'd be up to it?"

"Oh, I am! I am, I am!"

"Well then!" I clapped my hands together in delight, yanking Caleb's right hand along in the process. I could sense him trying to ignore me. "Who says we have to wait for them to pay us another visit? Come with me." I jerked my handcuffed arm and sent Caleb practically toppling off the counter he was sitting on. "Let's check out the mall directory to strategize and make sure this is going to work."

"Whoa—hold up now, hot dog girl," Caleb said. (I didn't.) "What are you up to? We're a 'we' now—not a 'you.' You can't just treat me like I'm the back end of a horse costume on Halloween. I get a vote here."

"This isn't a democracy!" I shouted back at him, yanking at his wrist as he stumbled to keep up. "You told me to leave you out of it, and I'm leaving you out of it. So just shut up, and keep up."

CHAPTER NINE

Make Yourself Ready . . .
For the Mischance of the Hour

Like a pair of witless zombies, Caleb and I lurched down the mall corridor until we finally synchronized our pace. Ariel flitted and skipped alongside us, über-eager to defend my honor. Part of me wondered how much of her enthusiasm was really just about getting the opportunity to be a belated participant in the high school sphere she had idealized from afar. My own petty, cliquish drama seemed a fascinating novelty to her, as impassioned and eyebrow-raising as a soap opera, minus the bad acting. I could see how an outsider might deem it all a welcome distraction from some of the more existential ponderings of adolescence: Doozies such as figuring out what you were supposed to do with your life, or weighing the likelihood that anything learned in trigonometry class would actually prove useful someday. The typical teen could be driven slowly insane by his or her own insipid inner monologues. Is it any wonder that we so readily devoured the sensational play-by-play and lurid gossip of the relationships that formed and/or splintered around us? Celebrity tabloid headlines seemed tame by comparison.

"Ow!" A painful pull on my arm yanked me back to the present.

"Oh, what? Did I breathe wrong again? Look, we're never going to be friends; that's a given," Caleb said, "but if we're going to be shackled together for the foreseeable future, we might as well try to get along, at least until I can find something to bust open these cuffs."

"Caleb's right," said Ariel. "You two really need to kiss and make up already."

"Never," I said, practically sputtering.

"It was just an expression, Miranda. Jeez," said my coworker.

"I'm pretty sure Tim Burton couldn't even think up this guy." I glared at the offending creature, who scowled before answering in turn.

"Some of the other kids may think you walk on water, her included." He pointed his thumb in the direction of Ariel, my arm flapping helplessly along for the ride. "But I see right through you. You're just a private school princess with an inflated ego. You can rule as demiurge over your little island of misfit toys, but you won't stand a chance in the real world."

"Socially inept *and* bitter," I said. "A winning combination you have there."

Looking over at Ariel, I saw that the expression on her face resembled that of a child told on Christmas morning that Santa hadn't made it this year because he and Mrs. Claus were embroiled in a messy divorce. No matter what I thought about Caleb (or what he thought about me), it wasn't worth raining on Ariel's parade. If the little sylph wanted to have some fun at the expense of my mortal enemies, I wasn't about to stand in her way. And if it proved cathartic for me in the process, well, what was the harm in that?

"Alrighty then," I said, turning to Caleb and holding out my free hand. "For the purposes of this evening's entertainment, I'll promise to be civil, if you will."

"Agreed," he said, sounding almost human, for once. "Besides, I'm a huge Tim Burton fan. I took that as a compliment." Of course he did.

"Great!" Ariel said, instantly cheerful once again. "Let the games begin!"

Just then Troy and Derek rounded the corner at full speed, nearly running into us, their arms loaded down with supplies.

"Hey, what's the big hurry?" Caleb wondered as they skidded to a halt.

"It's a full-on militia," Derek said, panting. "The Eastern Prep kids have dug in and set up a perimeter with BB guns."

"Can they do that?" said Ariel.

"Looks like they're doing whatever they want," answered Caleb, as Troy and Derek took their leave.

The news that Brian's posse had taken such ludicrously extreme—and potentially violent—measures to stake their so-called turf furthered my resolve to wreak a little havoc on them. They'd have to arm themselves with something more substantial than a BB gun to keep Miranda Prospero at bay. Their false bravado didn't scare me. Given what I had up my sleeve, they were the ones who should be nervous, I thought.

"Listen up," I said. "It's payback time." I gave Caleb and Ariel a cursory outline of my planned course of action, which, if I do say so myself, had the potential for restoring my legendary status.

"Wow," said Ariel, when I'd finished my spiel. "You just came up with that?"

"It's what I do," I said with what was probably a poor attempt at modesty. "Any questions?"

"Yeah, I have one," Caleb said. "You actually think these lame-brained plans are going to work?"

"Miranda knows what she's doing, Caleb. She's a mastermind. You'll see."

"This isn't *Unicorn Fantasy*, Ariel," he said.

"It's not like we have anything else to do," I said.

He sighed. "You do have a point there. Fine, I'll go along with this, but only out of curiosity. And, well. . . ." He glanced at our wrists, "because I'd have to gnaw my own arm off if I wanted to object."

"On the bright side, it couldn't taste any worse than your options at the food court." I noted a barely perceptible uptick in the corners of his mouth. Behold! The beast could smile! Speaking of beasts, I turned the corner and headed toward our first stop in this sojourn: the pet store.

"But I still don't understand," Ariel said a few minutes later. "It just seems cruel."

"Don't be such a softie. This is the same girl that started an anonymous group called 'Chub Club' and encouraged people to upload photos of any girls in our class who were perceived to be the least bit heavy. And let's not forget how she treated you a few hours ago at your party."

"I didn't mean cruel to *Rachel*," my coworker said. "I'm totally on board with that. I just don't understand why an itty bitty furball has to be exploited for the purpose."

"No animals will be harmed in the making of this poetic justice. It's PETA-approved, I assure you."

Caleb scoffed, but I refrained from putting him in his place since we had just entered the pet shop and had business to attend to. The store mostly dealt in small critters—fish, hamsters, newts, and the like. The place had that slightly off odor, a mixture of aquarium chemicals and gerbil pellets. Past the register, a mynah bird named Myrtle eyed us suspiciously from her spacious cage.

"Was*up*!!!" she trilled. Poor bird. Who taught her to talk like a drunk frat boy?

"Okay, Ariel," I said, ignoring Myrtle and walking toward a glass pen near the back of the store. "That white one with the wonky ear is perfect. Can you hold it for me until we're ready?"

Ariel's smile was so exuberant it looked poised to leap off her face.

"Can I name it?"

"Good lord." I knew it would be fruitless to talk her out of it. "Just make it snappy."

"No, not Snappy. She doesn't look like a Snappy. Awwww . . . hello, my sweet baby girl." She lifted the bunny tenderly from its pen and kissed it gently on its nose. She pondered its frankly creepy pinkish eyes before turning it upside down to cradle it in her arms like a baby. "Oh! Or should I say 'baby boy!' Well, now, you have an important mission, little guy, so you need a distinguished name. Nothing too obvious like Peter or Roger, but nothing *too* pretentious or hard to pronounce either, because—"

"Hurry up, Ariel."

"A name is important, Miranda! You can't rush me!"

"Yes I can. We don't have all night."

"Actually, we sort of do," Caleb said.

"Thank you, peanut gallery. Let's just get a move on it."

"Oh gosh," Ariel said, fretting. "I don't do my best work under pressure, but let's see . . . um, okay, how about Sebastian?"

"Sebastian? As in Johan?"

"No, as in *The Little Mermaid*." She turned to Caleb. "He was Ariel's sidekick, this funny little crab with a Jamaican accent. He almost gets boiled alive at one point and—"

"Super. Great. Fantastic," I said. "We now baptize thee Sebastian, blah-blah-blah," I made the sign of the cross over the powder puff in Ariel's arms. "Okay, the bunny's in business. Oh my god, this plan is the kind of stuff Stephen King dreams up."

"Stephen who?" Ariel looked at me, confused.

"You really think she reads horror novels?" Caleb chided me. "Don't worry about it, Ariel. You just stick to the Disney stuff."

"Never mind, both of you," I snapped. "We've got to figure out where Rachel is. She could be anywhere in the mall, though it's a safe bet she's still attached at the hip to Brian."

"You're one to talk," Caleb pointed out.

Ariel wandered off with Sebastian, cooing something about finding him some rabbit treats. I noticed Myrtle bobbing her neck forward and backward and sidestepping along her perch.

"Wassup! Wassup!" she chirped. Why did that sound so familiar?

"Oh. My. God." I instantly realized. "Brian was here."

"How do you know?" Caleb wondered.

"Myrtle. I'll explain later." I inched up to the bird cage. Hopefully my powers of persuasion were as effective on birds as they were on humans.

"Hi, pretty bird!"

"Wassup! " Uggh. I'd heard my fill of that phrase over the last two years.

"Yes, wassup! They were in here tonight, weren't they, you winged goddess?"

"Wassup! "

"Where did the mean boy and his bitchy girlfriend go? Did they say? Can you tell me where, smart birdy?"

Caleb tapped me on the shoulder with his free hand. "Um, excuse me? I wanna go on record here as saying this is getting a little worrisome."

"Not now," I hissed. "I'm busy."

"As you were, then. Carry on."

"Heyyyy Myrtle, Wassup . . . wassup. . . ." I said, trying to speak her language. "Did they say where they were going next?"

Like the avian world's very own Bird Whisperer, I stupidly spent the next several minutes trying to psychically connect with Myrtle, cajoling and pleading with her to enlighten me as to Rachel and Brian's whereabouts. Just when I was about to acknowledge the inanity of my efforts and concede Caleb's point, Ariel walked back from the front of the store, stroking Sebastian's soft ears.

"Sorry, Miranda. I know you're busy with Myrtle, so I hate to interrupt, but just thought you'd want to know I spotted Rachel walking into Veronica's Boudoir just now."

Caleb doubled over in laughter, forcing my left shoulder to dip involuntarily.

"Okay, Ariel, thanks," I said with a sigh, tempering my frustration at both my cohorts. "Tell Sebastian to get ready. It's on."

***

Veronica's Boudoir was on the mall's upper floor within close proximity to where the Eastern Preppies were bivouacked at this end of the building. That meant the payoff could be huge if my plan unfolded without a hitch. As we darted, unseen, from the pet shop toward the lingerie store, I quickly filled Ariel in on Rachel's history.

"She's from Poughkeepsie, not Manhattan like she claims. Her mom married the black sheep brother of the heir to a cough drop fortune when Rachel was in middle school and that's when they moved here. Her true roots are a bit more, well, rural."

"I don't get it," said Ariel confused. "How does that help us take her down a notch? And why do we need Sebastian?"

"Just wait," I said. "You'll see."

I thought back to the weekend I'd accidentally happened upon Rachel's inner demon, so to speak. She and the Itneys had conked out in front of the TV watching *SNL*. I couldn't sleep, and since I typically read in lieu of counting sheep, I went up to Rachel's room to grab *Jane Eyre* from my overnight bag. It wasn't where I left it, so I checked the closet to see if her housekeeper, Rosie, had hung it up in there. I'd been in her bank-vault-sized walk-in closet plenty of times before when we tried on outfits for double dates or the first day of school. I ventured back to where Rachel kept all her designer purses, stored with the same loving care as the Met's Egyptian collection. I couldn't find my bag, but on a shelf in the corner underneath a stack of *Vogues* I noticed a fabric-covered binder. It was about four inches thick, trimmed in a surfeit of white eyelet and pink ribbon. Curious, I picked it up, expecting to see cute pictures of Rachel as a baby. Turned out it wasn't a photo album but more of a scrapbook-journal hybrid put together by someone who couldn't have been much older than twelve or thirteen. Common decency would have dictated that I put the book back where I'd found it, but since most of this "young Rachel's" inner musings were surprisingly banal (names for her future children, celebrity crushes) I didn't feel too guilty about reading on. Nevertheless, by the time I'd emerged from Rachel's bedroom and snuggled back into my sleeping bag in the family room, I felt privy to a dark recess of her mind that I was certain she'd never meant to share with anyone.

Peering around the entrance to the boutique like a three-headed monster, Caleb, Ariel, and I saw Rachel in back browsing the bras and lace teddies. Having ascertained that our target was still there, we retreated out of her direct line of sight for a quick powwow.

"Okay, Ariel," I whispered, grabbing the thankfully placid rabbit from her and securing it in the crook of my free elbow. "We'll make sure Sebastian's in the right place at the right time. All you need to do is go in the store and tell Rachel that Brian is freaking out downstairs at Teasers wondering where she is. Escort her to the elevator, and keep her distracted. Press the button for the ground floor, then once the doors start to close, hit the alarm button. You've got to jump back out as fast as you can."

Having handed Ariel her marching orders, I headed to the nearby glass elevator with Caleb in tow.

"Sorry, genius, but pressing the alarm button isn't going to trap her in the elevator," he said.

"Duh! What do you take me for, a sociopath? I'm not going to trap her anywhere."

"Okay then, would you care to spell it out? Because you lost me."

"Don't I wish. Look, I'll explain it all later. Let's just get Little Bunny Foo-Foo in there. They should be heading this way any second."

I gently placed Sebastian on the corner of the elevator floor with a pile of Muesli-looking rabbit food to keep him from scampering out. Caleb and I hid out of view as the elevator closed in on him. My heart took five more pounding beats before Ariel and Rachel came walking at a fast shuffle around the corner.

"But like, what was he saying?" Rachel said. "Did he seem pissed? I mean, I *told* him where I'd be! And, no offense, but seriously? I don't need a nonentity like *you* getting involved."

"I just think you'd better go talk to him, ASAP," said Ariel, ignoring the blatant insult. When the elevator door opened, both girls stepped in, but not a half second later, my diminutive pal flitted back through the closing doors as the elevator's screeching alarm bell began to sound. Rachel's bloodcurdling scream soon chimed in. A masterstroke, if I do say so myself.

I'd discovered the unusual chink in Rachel's armor about halfway through my perusal of the doily-covered chronicle she'd stashed in her closet. She'd written passionate entries about her involvement with the 4-H club breeding and raising rabbits. (Embarrassing, right? But I digress.) One section of the binder served as a shrine-like documentation of her zealous commitment to her "beauties." I scanned through pictures of a chubby-cheeked, knobby-kneed Rachel posing proudly in front of her outdoor rabbit hutch, cradling baby rabbits as if she herself had carried them in her womb for nine months. Blue ribbons from county fairs were Scotch-taped alongside crude line graphs of the creatures' ages and weights written in Crayola markers. I could tell from the photos and her overuse of smiley faces and exclamation points, that her favorite rabbit was a pure white roly-poly guy she called Fritz. Clearly this had been no mere passing fancy but a hardcore obsession for Rachel. All of it was certainly understandable behavior from a prepubescent girl; quite sweet, really. But like *Charlotte's Web* minus the feel-good heroics of a literate arachnid, Rachel had to face the morbidly pragmatic reality: Most rabbits bred in captivity are not intended to live happily ever after. I didn't have to picture Rachel bawling her eyes out saying goodbye to a caged Fritz and friends the day they were sent off to, well, I shudder to think where. Her journal had elaborated on the heartrending scene in great detail.

And here's where things got weird. As the journal continued, Rachel began making fairly frequent references to nightmares involving Fritz. In the dreams, he started off looking docile and sweet as she'd known him, but he'd eventually manifest ferocious, razor-sharp teeth and an insatiable bloodlust. She'd wake in a cold sweat, and confided in her diary that she'd felt certain Fritz was haunting her as punishment for sending him to his dismal fate.

From an appreciable distance, Ariel, Caleb, and I watched Rachel make her screaming descent in the glass elevator. Midway between the upper and lower floors, the transparent box came to a sudden halt. Rachel was hysterically pushing buttons on the elevator panel, banging frantically on the buttons, doors, and glass window panes.

"Well, what do you know. She *is* stuck!" Caleb said.

"That wasn't my doing," I said. "She must have accidentally hit the emergency stop button in her desperation to get out."

By this point, the elevator alarm bell and Rachel's screams had drawn a growing number of bemused looky-loos from the cool-kids' ground floor camp. A chorus of "holy shit"s and "what's she doing?"s echoed staccato-like up to the second floor from where we stealthily watched the proceedings.

Still stuck between floors, Rachel flattened her back up against the side of the elevator opposite Sebastian, whom I could just barely see nibbling nonchalantly on bunny kibble. She kept craning her head to look away from the bunny, writhing and squinting her eyes as if she was facing a nuclear blast.

"Nooooooo!" she screamed. Her hyperventilating chest heaved up and down, like some sort of beleaguered heroine in a high-octane action flick. "Let me outuuuut! He's going to steal my soul! He's going to steal my SOUL!!! Somebody, please! Save me!"

I stared wide-eyed—the histrionics were way better than even I had predicted—while Ariel watched amazed, her hand cupped over her glimmering orthodontia.

Finally, Brian emerged from the crowd that was gathered ten feet or so below the elevator car. "Rachel!" he said, half shouting, half chuckling. "Was*sup*, babe!?"

His flunkies all laughed hysterically while Rachel just stared down and wailed, big fat tears cascading over her cheeks. By the time they'd all stopped teasing her and instructed her to simply push the ground floor button so the elevator would resume operation, she looked stark raving mad. She raced out when she reached the ground floor, and the doors shut behind her. Ariel crept unseen to call the elevator back up so we could retrieve Sebastian and return him safe and sound to the pet shop.

***

As we walked back in that direction, I filled Ariel and Caleb in on Rachel's history with Fritz.

"Wow, straight out of *Donnie Darko*," Caleb remarked. "I have to admit—not that I'm condoning it or anything, but—that was truly something to behold."

I blushed with pride. Normally, I would have spent the next hour (well, make that the next week) reveling in my *coup de grace*, but my work here wasn't finished. Not by a long shot.

"Hey, did either of you see Britney or Whitney down there among all the gawkers?" Ariel and Caleb both shook their heads no.

"Okay then, let's drop off Sebastian and motor," I said. "I think I know where we might find them."

CHAPTER TEN

They'll Take Suggestion as a Cat Laps Milk

"Work it, girl," Britney said as Whitney half-tripped over her own feet, clad in six-inch leopard-print heels. She collapsed into a cushy armchair and made a cavalier show of kicking the prized pumps off her feet. One landed with a rustle in the tissue-papered box on the floor but the other missed its mark, alighting next to one of several crumpled piles of clothing. Removing a pair of ginormous Jackie O. sunglasses—the $320 price tag still dangling from the frame—Whitney looked at them with passing interest before tossing them over her shoulder.

"This is about as boring as, like, a medically induced coma," she said, sighing. "I can't believe I'm actually saying this, but I'm sick of trying on clothes."

"That's a first," said Britney, grabbing a pink cocktail dress off a nearby rack and holding the hanger up to her chest. "Would you say this color is 'bubble gum' or 'baboon butt?'" When Whitney ignored her, she rolled her eyes, dropped the dress and its hanger to the floor, and stepped lithely over it. "Okay, then. What do *you* want to do?"

"Let's go meet back up with *Brian.*" Whitney's voice was a grating squawk, and paired with her overdone eye makeup and "Sweet Sixteen" nose job, she reminded me of a colorful macaw parrot.

"I got the impression Rachel wanted us to bail for a while. You know—for some, like, alone time."

"Yeah, whatever," Whitney said. She and her rhyming counterpart had boyfriends who, like Rachel's ex, Max, had left for college in the fall.

Caleb, Ariel, and I watched the two of them from the mezzanine above the dress salon at Blumenfelds. The place looked like it'd been ransacked, strewn with frocks hung over the backs of chairs and in piles in front of the three-way mirror. Rachel, the Itneys, and I had tried on gowns here for homecoming last year. It was hard to reconcile that not-too-distant memory with the present moment, but I'll admit I had fun at the time. And why not? We were four fetching girls with expensive tastes, hot boyfriends, and enough money to buy pretty much whatever we wanted. Not a care in the world, and, I could finally see in hindsight, not a clue.

I turned to Ariel and gave her a single nod. She solemnly nodded in return before taking the back staircase from the mezzanine down to where the Itneys were pulling on their knee-high leather boots. My coworker, smiling beatifically, acted as though she'd stumbled on them completely by accident. Her acting—hardly the stuff of Meryl Streep—made me cackle, but Caleb gently elbowed me and I managed to stifle it.

"What are *you* doing here?" Whitney asked, her expression more befitting someone who'd just sniffed a carton of sour milk. "You work with Miranda at that nauseating hot dog stand, don't you?"

"Um, yeah, that would be me," she said, looking appropriately cowed, like we'd practiced.

"What do you want?" asked Britney.

"Well, I heard that people from your school were glam-camping on this end of the mall, with actual cots and gourmet coffee and stuff," Ariel said, talking too fast. "The food court is like a trailer park after a tornado, and Miss Know-It-All Miranda thinks she's running the place. I'm totally sick of her ordering me around. I'm looking to defect."

The Itneys didn't respond. I glanced nervously at Caleb, but Ariel had already taken a different tack. "Gorgeous dresses, huh?" she said, surveying the scene. "How much did they pay you?"

"Huh?" Britney looked confused.

"Well, you're models, aren't you? From the mini fashion show they put on here this afternoon? I mean, you're both skinny and gorgeous, so I just put two and two together. . . ." Ariel followed this up with a winning smile. Nicely done. The Itneys loved a sycophant, as I'd explained to her earlier. They would eat this up.

"You know, without that stupid hot dog hat, you're actually less of a dorkus than I originally thought," Britney said, tact never being her strong suit. "Your eye makeup actually looks, like, pretty professional closeup."

"Oh, this?" Ariel gave a modest smile. "I experimented a little with it earlier tonight since there was nothing better to do."

"Huh," Whitney said. "It's amazing the miracles makeup can achieve."

Ariel changed the subject, all cherubic innocence.

"So, which one of you is dating that hottie, Brian?"

"Uh . . . neither of us," said Britney, giving her counterpart a sideways glance. "He and Rachel are together."

"No way," Ariel said, aghast. "But I thought he'd be with one of you, for sure!"

"That's just what we were saying!" Whitney looked put out. "What does she have that we don't? We're cuter, thinner, and we dress better."

"It's never going to work out between them," added Britney.

"Why, does he like someone else?" asked Ariel.

Whitney got a knowing smirk on her face—what did *that* mean? More importantly, when was Ariel going to get on with it and make her move already?

"Speaking of models," said my coworker. "Did you guys hear about that app called CopperPhone? It emits an ultraviolet laser from your cell phone that actually gives you a tan if you wave it over your skin." Caleb and I exchanged defeated glances. This wasn't the plan! Not even the Itneys were dumb enough to buy that load of crap.

"For real?!" Whitney said. Britney dug into her huge leather satchel and pulled out her phone in its pink bejewelled case. She swiped her forefinger across the screen frantically.

"Still no connection. Damn."

"Oh here," Ariel said. "I can show you on mine." She pulled her own cell phone from the front pocket of her smock and poked around at the screen while Whitney sniveled about being trapped all night without her full retinue of beauty products.

"God, I need my bedtime detox mask, or my face will be, like, an oil slick in the morning," she said, simpering.

"Tell me about it," said Britney. "I was hoping to touch up my roots before we leave for Aspen tomorrow. *If* we even get to go, that is."

Ariel handed her phone to Britney. "See. Just push this button here to activate the UV laser. Then you glide it over your skin like so."

"Shut the front door!" Britney slid the phone over her arms and neck like it was a bar of soap before glancing skeptically at Ariel. "But wait . . . you're like, an albino."

"I know, stupid Germanic genes. Isn't it, like, *tragic?*" Hearing Ariel mimic their snobby patois was cracking me up. "Why do you think I downloaded it this morning? It's supposed to take, like, a few days before you really start to see the effects."

"Fake-and-bake on the go? This is, like, effing brilliant!" Whitney said. Caleb turned to me, slackjawed. I nodded, equally astonished. It was obvious (to us, at least) that Ariel's "UV laser" was just a run-of-the-mill flashlight app. But this wasn't part of our game plan, and time was of the essence, especially now that Britney had hoisted her handbag over her shoulder, clearly ready to shove off.

"Thanks for the tip, kid. Hey, Whit, let's go troll Main Street for a while." They were about to walk out on Ariel with nary a backward glance when my colleague called after them. This was her last chance to springload the trap.

"You know, I could get you into Blissworks Body if you wanted, for a couple of spa treatments."

Both girls spun around faster than the Tasmanian Devil. Britney eyed her suspiciously.

"But how? Everyone there went home early on account of the snow. The gate's already down."

"Oh, I thought you knew! I'm in the Blissworks trainee program," Ariel explained. "A girl can't sell hot dogs for the rest of her life, you know. I've been taking beauty classes over there on my days off."

"You?!" said Whitney in disbelief.

"Actually, I was just over there fixing myself up. I don't think they'd mind if I used you as practice clients. I could touch up your highlights, too, Britney."

Naturally, all this was a lie. The reality was, the Blissworks stockroom door opened onto the same utility corridor that led to our back hallway at the food court. Ariel and I frequently ran free Diet Cokes down to the Blissworks staff, so they'd given us their door code to get in through the back when they were busy with clients. From there, all Ariel had to do was grab the key from their front counter to open up the front gate.

None the wiser, the Itneys briefly conferred before noddingly accepting her servitude.

"Okay, then!" Ariel said. "I've got a few things I need to take care of first, so why don't you meet me out in front of Blissworks in, like, an hour? Toodles!"

By the time Caleb and I descended from the mezzanine, Ariel looked like a Golden Retriever who'd just fetched us a pair of slippers.

"Boy were they clueless," she said.

"*CopperPhone?!?*" I said.

"I know, it was off-the-cuff," Ariel said. "But I could tell they weren't biting. I needed to think of something."

"Okay, okay. You've certainly proved you can handle Dumb and Dumber, so I'll let you take the lead on this one. Go ahead and get down to the spa. We'll meet back at home base when you're done with them. In the meantime, I've got one more fish to fry." I yanked on Caleb's wrist. "*Vamanos.*"

While Ariel departed toward Blissworks, Caleb and I started out on our own.

"So he dumped you and then took up with your best friend?" He was trying to get up to speed on the facts as we traipsed as a pair back down the mall. "I get the whole 'scorned woman' thing, but isn't this a little much? And what did those two girls do to you, anyway?"

"There's a lot more to it. I know it seems a little petty, but trust me when I say that Ariel and I are doing a service to mankind tonight. And I haven't even settled the big score yet."

"Ever heard the phrase 'Let bygones be bygones?'"

"Ever heard the phrase 'Mind your own business?'"

"I've been trying to, believe me," Caleb said with a sigh. "But you're not making it easy dragging me on your special-ops missions. I'd like nothing better than to just be chilling out at the food court. Besides which, I'm starving."

"You're hungry?"

"Well, yeah. I've only eaten a piece of birthday cake in the last twelve hours."

"I'm hungry, too," I conceded. "Okay, we'll take a quick food break. But that *doesn't* mean I'm letting Brian off the hook."

"I believe you."

"C'mon then. I know where you can get a mean corn dog."

Back at ground zero, the tables and chairs of the food court had all been stacked against the perimeters, leaving a wide open expanse of floor. Chad and Dex, appropriately attired in their Cleat Locker uniforms, were officiating a bizarre sporting match of sorts. A maze of plastic "wet floor" sandwich signs were arrayed as obstacles on the playing field while team members stood in empty yellow mop buckets on caster wheels. (Every stall in the food court had their own.) Troy whizzed past us in his bucket.

"Hey, Miranda!" He propelled himself forward with the business end of a cotton rope mop. The objective, from what I could tell, involved using the self-same mops to bat a ten-pound bag of ice across the floor into the opposing team's goal. These were demarcated by the red velvet ropes and chrome stanchions with which the movie theater managed lines.

Caleb and I must have looked absolutely stupified, because Dex offered up a quick tutorial as he trotted past with his ref's whistle. "Inverted ice hockey meets polo meets quidditch. The team that scores the most before the ice melts wins." Boy, these people really *were* bored.

As Caleb took in the action, I noticed Quinn a few feet away lying on the counter at Paisano's. Her casual comportment aside, she looked stricken.

"What's wrong, Red?" I asked. "Don't you feel well?" Her titian ponytail hung off the side of the counter glumly.

"I'm just worried. Mike's been missing all night and I *know* something's wrong. No one seems to care!"

"We do care, I promise! Like I told you before, I'm sure he just went home early. I know you haven't spoken to him, but once phones are up and running, you'll find out he's been vegging on the couch watching some Will Ferrell movie marathon or something."

"But he didn't leave! I can see from the mall entrance that his Jeep Cherokee is still in the lot."

"The roads are gnarly; he probably caught a ride with someone."

"His Jeep can get through snow better than most cars. Besides, he would have told me he was taking off."

I'd been acquainted with Mike only in passing during my brief tenure as a mall employee. I barely knew the guy, which left me at a loss for any real words of encouragement.

"Grady was down here about a half-hour ago checking in on us," Quinn said. "There's been no sign of Mike on the security monitors in his office, but he said he'd keep looking while he's making the rounds."

"Speaking of MIAs," said Derek, interrupting, "Troy and I got separated from Colin on our supply run and I don't think he's been back this way since."

"Hell," said Troy, "those Eastern Prep kids have all the good stuff, including Teasers' 'sub-prime' rib. Maybe he decided to switch teams."

"You mean in the gay sense?" Alfredo shook his head in disagreement. "No way. Though that clown costume does suggest he's at least bi-curious."

"Let's not start slamming people's uniforms," I said. "Anyway, I'm sure it's nothing. Knowing Colin he's just back at Cheeze Monkey trying to claim the all-time highest score in Skee-Ball."

"I don't know, man." Troy returned us to the subject at hand. "This is beginning to seem like one of those godawful teen horror movies where one by one everyone disappears . . . and *dies*."

"Oh, come on."

"No, I'm serious! People are missing, and that computer store thief is probably still out there somewhere."

Caleb inched a step closer to me. "He's right," he whispered for my ears only. "And Ariel's out there, too."

CHAPTER ELEVEN

Now I Will Believe That There Are Unicorns

There seemed to be a nervous undercurrent rippling through the food court crowd. To subdue my keyed-up minions, I suggested a cook-off competition for anyone interested and divvied workers into teams and a panel of judges.

"The first challenge? Invent a new frozen yogurt flavor using only ingredients available at any of the food stalls," I said. Teams set to work crumbling fortune cookies from Wok 'Dis Way and experimenting with a less-than-promising barbecue-chocolate flavor combo. This was going to create even more of a mess than we'd already managed, but *c'est la vie*.

While I cast a weary eye over my surroundings, I felt the faintest urge, one that sent shivers of dread down my spine: I needed to pee. I mentally commanded my bladder to stand down, having no other option at present.

"Dude, we would have killed it tonight," Chad said, banging his hand against the wall Caleb was leaning against. "You would have totally blown minds with your sweep picking."

"Sold out show, too. Though I guess it doesn't matter now."

I glanced over at the guys. Curious? Yes. Willing to admit it? No.

"Wonder if that cougar superfan would have been front-and-center again," Chad said, chuckling. "Are you curating her thong collection?"

"Who said she was aiming for me?" Caleb replied.

"Okay, um, I'm sorry," I said, no longer able to act disinterested. "Please tell me you are not into women's underwear." Silence. "Caleb?"

"We were supposed to play a gig," Chad said, answering for him. "This guy is a living legend."

"What guy?" I was so confused.

"Your right-hand man here. Or," the pretty boy scrutinized our wrists more closely, "I guess he'd be your 'left-hand' man."

I turned to Caleb. "What's he talking about?"

"Exactly what he said. We were supposed to play a gig tonight."

"You're in a band. Isn't that precious?" I said, envisioning amateur hour in his parents' garage. "What do you call yourselves?"

"The Drunk Butlers," Chad interrupted. "I'm on drums. Caleb's our 'Bono,' if you will."

"If Bono played guitar like The Edge," Caleb said.

"The Drunk Butlers?"

Caleb nodded, stonefaced.

"*The* Drunk Butlers?"

"Maybe you've heard us," Chad said. "We've been getting air time for the past few weeks on KLMN and a few of the college indie stations. We were supposed to play tonight at the El Beau Theater."

"Oh my God! I thought you looked familiar!" Brooke had apparently been eavesdropping and now chimed in. "My cousin Hannah has a picture of you guys taped up in her locker. She's freakin' obsessed with 'Past Is Prologue.' Awesome song, by the way."

"Thanks," said Caleb, eking out a smile. I ignored Chad and Brooke both, and stared dumbfounded at Caleb.

"Now I've heard everything," I said.

"What can I say? I'm full of surprises."

Forty-five minutes later the guys were still milking the thwarted rock star routine for all it was worth; Caleb, acting more animated than I'd seen him all night, practiced frets on an imaginary guitar neck with his free hand while Chad indulged in impromptu bursts of drumming using a set of chopsticks from Wok 'Dis Way. I caught myself glancing alternately between them, as if watching a too-evenly matched game of televised tennis, and realized we had sunk to a new nadir of boredom at "base camp." At this rate, it was going to be a long night, unless. . . . The words "tennis," "match," and "love" kick-started the synapses firing in my brain and I sprang, if not literally, at least mentally, into action.

"Chad," I said, "I'm worried about Ariel. I mean she's out there all alone—"

"Thanks to you and your special brand of vigilante justice," Caleb said under his breath. I found that with time, I was getting better at ignoring him.

"She's so small and defenseless and you're obviously—"

"Miranda, do you really need to lay it on so thick?" said Caleb. "If you want him to go help Ariel, why don't you just try asking him?"

"That's what I'm *doing* if you'd stop interrupting me!"

"I mean without all the eyelash batting. Not everything has to be a game of Mistress Manipulation."

"Whatever," I said, then looked at Chad expectantly. "You'll go look for her, right?"

"Sure." He blushed, per usual. "I still don't get what she's doing way down at the spa place, but I can go check on her."

After Chad headed down the hall, Caleb and I tried joining another game of "ice hockey" in progress, but since we couldn't figure out a feasible way to move in tandem without potentially breaking our necks, Caleb suggested we try something more cerebral, like a game of chess. I admitted I didn't know how to play.

"You're kidding me," he said, looking at me as if I didn't know how to tie my own shoelace. "Well, you know what that means. Class is now in session."

Without caring whether or not I was up for being his pupil, he grabbed the travel chess case he'd gifted Ariel and proceeded to set it up at the table farthest away from the ice hockey game. I watched closely as Caleb arranged the pieces on the board with his free hand, naming each one, from the pawn all the way up to the king.

"Can we call this thing something other than 'bishop?'" I wondered, pointing to one of the pieces with a domed top. "That's my diabolical ex-boyfriend's last name." Caleb rolled his eyes at me.

"Get over it. We're not going to start assigning pet names to the game pieces just to humor your whole he-done-me-wrong routine."

"All right! Jeez. I didn't realize you'd get all pedantic about it."

"There are other fish in the sea, you know."

"Nice. Which book of clichés did you plagiarize that from?"

Caleb ignored me and started explaining the intricate rules of the game, including pointing out the properties of the different chess pieces.

"You'd assume it's the king—because that's who you have to defeat to win—but the queen is actually the most powerful piece in the entire game." He turned the white queen in his hand as he spoke, his eyes locked on mine as if to impress his point. "She's the only one that can move to any number of unoccupied squares in any direction: vertically, horizontally, or diagonally."

"Right on," I said. "Chicks rock."

"*Sometimes*," he seemed to grudgingly concede.

"Oh, give me a break. Don't try to pretend your whole 'I'm with the band' schtick isn't just an elaborate ruse to score with the ladies. How's that working for you, anyway? Does the thong-throwing cougar light your fire, or are you just waiting for your diehard teeny-bopper groupies to come of age?"

"You play me false," he said. "I don't write songs to stoke my love life. Though if it's a happy byproduct of my endeavors, then so be it."

"As if I care about your love life," I said—though, truthfully, I was a little curious. "Let's focus on the game."

He ran me through a couple of classic opening strategies with names like the Sicilian Defense and the Latvian Gambit, and then we began. I quickly determined that it was like no other game I'd ever played. Checkers was mere tic-tac-toe compared to the seemingly endless combination of mental moves and manipulations that could lead either to conquest or capture. I thrilled to the inherent challenge of it. If I really wanted to learn, I'd have to be patient and practice just as if I were learning to play a musical instrument or a foreign language.

"The key to winning is patience," Caleb said, as if reading my thoughts. I had just lost another bishop to one of his pawns. "You always have to think a few steps ahead and stay focused on your goal."

I was so intent on the game at hand, that when Ariel and Chad appeared at the entrance to the food court I realized I'd forgotten to be annoyed with Caleb and, instead, found myself awed by his skill. But now, my protégé was waving excitedly, as though she'd just brought home Olympic gold.

"Miranda, we did it! This is the most fun I've had since Epcot World," she said. "I never thought giving a makeover could be so personally fulfilling."

"Details. Tell me everything!"

"Well, I started by giving Britney some new 'highlights,'" Ariel said. "She asked for honey blonde. I went for something more puce."

"Ew."

"Whitney asked for a Brazilian blowout, and boy, did I give her one. Her hair is now a total frizz bomb!"

"I always thought she'd make a good Bride of Frankenstein. So, what else, what else?"

"Well, I convinced them I had an expensive new anti-cellulite cream. They begged me to slather it on, having no idea it was . . . drumroll, please. . . ." Chad readily obliged while she paused dramatically. ". . . henna tattoo dye!"

"You didn't!" I said with a squeal.

"Oh, but I did!" Ariel squealed back, as we both jumped up and down.

"Oh my god, Ariel," I said. "Well done, young grasshopper. Seems I totally underestimated your abilities."

"Your suggestion of putting cucumbers on their eyelids was brilliant. They couldn't see a thing."

"I showed up just as Ariel was exiting," said Chad. "I had no idea what was happening, but she hightailed it outta there, so I just tried to keep up."

"Thanks for having my back," Ariel said, beaming at him adoringly.

"No problem," Chad answered, his face still flush. "High-maintenance chicks never were my thing."

"Okay, well, we can reasonably assume that the Itneys will be busy for at least the next hour or so trying to repair the damage—"

A loud crash interrupted my thought and we all turned to see Dex sprawled on the floor next to an overturned table. He was quickly surrounded by several concerned teammates.

"I think I broke it," he said, groaning. Riley and Brooke put his arms over their shoulders and moved him, limping, over to a bench. Chad leaned down to take a look and ran a hand over Dex's ankle.

"I don't think so," he said. "More likely just a bad sprain of the anterior talofibular." He responded to our collective looks of surprise with a nonchalant shrug. "I'm planning to study sports medicine in college. This is basic first aid stuff. Speaking of, do you guys have a first aid kit down here? We should put some ice on this and wrap it up."

"Yeah, there's one next to Randall's desk," Ariel said. "I'll get it."

We made Dex as comfortable as possible with some of the blankets and pillows Troy and Derek had picked up on their supply run. When Ariel returned from Randall's office, she had a grim look on her face and held the yellowish plastic box open for our inspection.

"This thing probably hasn't been used in over a decade," she said. "There are some rusty safety pins and a few Band-Aids. That's it."

"Typical Randall," I said. "But don't worry, Dex. A few of us will head over to Worthington's and see if they'll kindly grant us a first aid kit."

"Maybe we could get them to throw in a pair of crutches, too." Ariel said.

"Do we have anything we could barter?" I added as an afterthought, though I doubted it would be necessary.

"Wow. You're actually considering going on a humanitarian mission rather than one of revenge?" said Caleb, one eyebrow raised in disbelief. "That's new."

"Believe it or not, most of my 'missions,' as you call them, *are* for selfless reasons. But since you don't know me *at all*, you wouldn't understand."

"I'll believe it when I see it," said Caleb. "I'd bet serious money you have an ulterior motive for this."

"Well, lucky for me I couldn't care less what you think and as for 'serious money,' if you had any, I doubt you'd be wasting your time working at a magic store. Ariel, can you and Troy pull together some portable snacks?"

"Why would they want our crappy food when they've got access to Teasers' steaks and fully loaded baked potatoes?" Ariel asked.

"Junk food is its own currency in the realm of teenage guys. Just grab a couple dozen bags of Funyuns from Sub Zero. I can't do anything while I'm manacled to this . . . this vile miscreant."

"You're the one who handcuffed us together, princess."

"You're the one who said *they weren't real.*"

"Guys, guys," said Ariel. "Enough, already. We're supposed to be helping Dex, remember? Let's go. But if my salon clientele are back down there, I'm going to need a human shield."

The "delegation"—Chad, Ariel, Caleb, and I—headed down the hall toward Worthington's while I silently lambasted my unwilling sidekick. I couldn't believe I'd considered for even a minute that the two of us might be able to see past our differences long enough to stop feuding. He clearly pegged me for a narcissistic brat, but I was through trying to defend myself. Perhaps I'd been a stuck-up princess before my downfall, but even at my very worst, my motives weren't diabolical, just selfish and thoughtless. Maybe it was sort of a cosmic joke that I was shackled to someone so misanthropic and judgmental he could only see the worst in me. If so, I wasn't laughing. My only option as I saw it was to continue along as though I didn't have this Shrek-wannabe at my side.

"Hold up." Caleb brought us all to a sudden stop, as if to remind me just how impossible ignoring him would be. With his free hand, he pointed toward Worthington's. There, a ginger-haired Eastern Prep kid, Harrison Temple, who went by the apt sobriquet "Prince Harry," sat in a beach chair thumbing through a comic book. A BB gun rested on his knees. Two other kids I didn't recognize were armed and stationed at either end of the giant drugstore's entrance. They both wore letterman jackets.

"Jeez," Chad said. "They really are guarding the perimeter."

"I'm sure they're just getting their kicks pretending to play G.I. Joe," I said. "It's not like they'd actually be stupid enough to use them."

"You're probably right, but better safe than sorry," Caleb said. "Let's be cautious. I don't want to spend any part of this already lame-ass night using tweezers to remove a BB pellet from one of your rear ends." As we approached, Prince Harry tossed the comic aside, stood up, and slung the BB gun over his shoulder. I was surprised he didn't have camo greasepaint on his face and a military beret.

"Hey, bro," Caleb said, "We've got a man down on our end. We're looking for a first aid kit."

"Hang on a sec," he said, unclipping a walkie talkie from his waistband. "It's Miranda Prospero," he glanced up and down my Hot-Dog Kabob threads. "And co. They want a first aid kit." He paused, then asked "What do you need it for?"

"What does it matter? We just need it," Caleb answered. "C'mon, man. Be cool. We have a guy with a sprained ankle."

"Leave this to me," I said under my breath to Caleb. I turned to Prince Harry. "Harrison, right? We hung out at Rachel Alonso's house that time last winter." If I remembered correctly Prince Harry ended the evening by driving his dad's Jaguar into a tree, but I decided not to mention that.

"Yeah, so?"

"So, I'm asking you if we can have the first aid kit—and maybe some pain reliever—as a personal favor. We even brought some snacks as a friendly gesture." I smiled in what I hoped was an ingratiating manner and ushered Ariel forward with the box of junk food we'd brought with us. She held up a bag of Funyuns and shook it temptingly.

"Duh. Worthington's has a whole aisle of crap like this. Why would we need your stupid little peace offering? Still, I guess we *could* give you a first aid kit—" Harrison turned and eyed the store behind him.

". . . But then we'd have to kill you," said a familiar voice. Brian Bishop had just materialized from behind a display rack of greeting cards and was now standing next to Harrison. Not only were his attempts at humor bad, they were cliché beyond belief.

"Handcuffs, eh?" he said, eyeing Caleb and me. "Kinky. If I'd known you were into bondage, maybe we'd still be dating. Speaking of our past, isn't it ironic that we're spending the night under the same roof?"

"Try looking up irony in the dictionary before you go throwing it around like you know what you're talking about. No wonder you needed someone else to take your SATs for you."

"If I were you, I'd set the Funyuns down," Brian said to Ariel.

"I don't take orders from you," she said with false bravado.

"Suit yourself. All I'm saying is, you'll need your hands free. . . ." He nodded at Harrison, who aimed the BB gun straight at us. ". . . so you can run faster. Ready, aim, fire!"

The first BB gun pellet hit the wall behind Chad's head, Ariel dropped the box, and we took off running. Survival instinct must've kicked in to help us sync up, because, for once, Caleb and

I were able to match our paces evenly until we were safely out of shooting range.

"Everyone okay?" Chad asked when we rounded the corner and paused to catch our breath.

"That's it!" I said, bending over and gasping for air.

"They are so going down," Ariel and I said in unison.

CHAPTER TWELVE

The Rarer Action Is in Virtue Than in Vengeance

We booked it back to the food court to regroup. The gearheads had finally stopped experimenting with Diet Coke and Mentos and were diverting themselves with a remote-controlled helicopter.

"We found a kit at Craftworks," said Raj, who normally worked a nearby cell phone kiosk. He stashed a retractable pencil in the pocket of his navy blue button-down shirt. "Mere mortals would require at least a week to assemble this baby. We figured it out in twenty-five minutes. Dude, ease up on the throttle! Ease up! You're going to ditch it!"

Grady was among those watching the chopper climb and dive over our heads, but when he saw me he casually ambled over.

"I was waiting for you to get back. Everyone's acting like you're de facto in charge over here, so word to the wise: Management's not going to take kindly to the mess down here."

It *did* look like a disaster zone, but what were they going to do, fire us? These minimum wage fast-food service jobs were nearly impossible to fill. I ignored Grady and addressed more pressing issues.

"You don't happen to have a set of handcuff keys?" I asked.

"Negatory. They rescinded our access to handcuffs here after the Cabbage Patch riots got ugly back in '83."

"I take it you don't have a sidearm, either."

Grady scoffed.

"Why on earth would you ask?"

"Well, have you been down to the other end of the mall lately? It's like the North Korean border!"

"Yeah, yeah, I've gotten a few complaints about that."

"And? Can't you do something?"

Grady scratched his head and shifted uncomfortably. It occurred to me that as the all-too-frequent butt of teenagers' jokes he might be particularly reticent about interacting with that elitist end of the mall.

"Look, Miranda, they're all pretty well corralled down there. Just give 'em a wide berth and they shouldn't be any trouble."

"Dude, they shot at us with BB guns," Caleb interrupted angrily. "Why should they get to occupy an entire annex of the building? They're not even mall employees."

"Calm down, calm down," Grady said, raising both arms defensively. "There's not much I can do here on my own. I don't foresee they're going to pose any problem so long as they confine themselves to that end. And I'd advise the same to all of you," he said, raising his voice as he scanned the room. "By morning the roads and parking lot should be cleared enough to let you all go home. But until then, no more running around the building willy-nilly. It's just not safe, and I can't be in ten places at once to keep an eye on you."

After glancing disinterestedly at the mall cop, everyone pretty much ignored him and went about their business.

"I don't suppose you've seen any sign of Mike?" I asked Grady as he turned to go.

"Can't say as I have."

"We're also missing a clown named Colin."

"See, that's exactly why you all need to just stay put," he said with a sigh. "I'll keep an eye out for them. Be back in an hour or so to check in."

Caleb watched Grady exit the food court before turning to me.

"I can't believe he won't do a damn thing about the Sons of Anarchy down there," he muttered. "They shouldn't be able to get away with that crap."

"For once, you and I are in agreement. But what are we supposed to do about it?"

"Don't look at me. Isn't that your specialty?"

He was right. This was exactly the sort of thing I was supposed to be good at. And yet here I was, stumped. And tired. And, wow; I really needed to pee. Is this how a sitting president felt midway through the first term? I used to get a little rush every time I got to work my magic, so to speak, but the responsibility was starting to weigh too heavily. Everyone looked to me to solve their problems, but who did I get to lean on when I needed help? This whole "playing God" thing was getting to be exhausting. I glanced up at the helicopter circling the ceiling and a synapse fired in my brain. Like Caleb said, I *was* really good at this, and well, one last hurrah might not be a bad thing.

"Hey, Raj," I said, raising my voice above the toy's loud whirring. "Were there any more of those helicopter kits?"

"Yeah, sure. Why?"

"Grab some of your guys. We're going back to Craftworks."

***

We brought everything back to the food court to assemble. My team of junior engineer wannabes huddled together, hard at work on building six more copters (and a few *Star Wars* RC X-Wing Fighters—they'd insisted) while the rest of us squeezed out dozens of bottles of glue into plastic sandwich baggies. Ariel, no surprise, had already tapped into the cases of glitter we'd found in bulk. She shook a handful into her palm, threw it up in the air, and looked enchanted as it fell flickering around her.

"Yo, Tinkerbell," I said, teasing her. "Don't OD on the pixie dust. We need it for the bombs."

Raj approached me with a progress report on the modifications he and his friends were working on.

"We superglued 'L' hooks to the underbellies. If we reverse direction fast enough in the air, the bombs should slide off and generally land in the vicinity of where we want 'em. Did I tell you what a bang-up idea this is by the way?"

"About twelve times already. But thanks. Let me know when everything's ready on your end."

"You know," said Caleb later, holding open a baggie with his free hand while I emptied a bottle of glue into it with my right. "This is pretty much an overt declaration of war. It's going to be a lot harder, after this, to carry out your stealth prank on Brian, whatever it is."

"Yeah, I know," I said. "But I'm considering making this my swan song. I've had an epiphany interacting with those a-holes tonight and am finally starting to see that I'm better off now than I was before; well, apart from the whole being saddled to your sorry butt all night. There's been *nothing* fun about that."

"The feeling is mutual. Hey, there we go again, agreeing on things." He paused for a moment. "Still, I would have loved to have seen whatever grand scheme you had planned for your ex. Your mind can be a scary-yet-enthralling place."

"Aha! I *knew* you were secretly loving our spy games," I said, ribbing him with both our elbows. "But yeah, it's weird. I thought I was angry at Brian, and don't get me wrong—he's a total lowlife. But I think the person I'm most fed up with is myself. What could I have possibly seen in that creep? In any of them?"

Caleb silently shrugged, scooping a pile of pink glitter and adding it to the glue-filled baggie. How maddening. Here I am chastened and contrite, and he says nothing, a silent acknowledgment that, yes, I'm a detestable diva. Then again, he didn't use the opportunity to make another one of his sardonic remarks. For someone who can read most people like a flimsy paperback novel, I still couldn't figure this guy out.

For obvious reasons, everyone wanted to come along when we executed our strike, which made me wary.

"I don't want anyone getting hurt, so don't get too close. For any of you filming it on your phones, just stay alert." I gave these orders to our rag-tag commandos as we approached the intersection between Worthington's and Teasers, the site where we could get the most Eastern Prep kids all at once. "The plan is to catch them off guard, but if they open fire, everyone needs to fall back."

Our glitter bomb blitzkrieg would only have been more exciting had a forty-piece orchestra been playing Wagner's "Ride of the Valkyries" as a soundtrack in the background. Instead, the buzzing clamor of the model aircraft drowned out the music that was emanating from Teasers and was enough to draw pretty much everyone from their encampment. I recognized a few of the kids as the same ones who'd badmouthed me when I'd first arrived at the food court at the beginning of my shift. Brian and Prince Harry were in the thick of it, craning their necks at the choppers with bemused, "That's the best you can do?" smirks. As soon as one bomb dropped, I knew the spectators would disperse, so the plan was to drop them all on one command. I didn't see Rachel or the Itneys in the crowd yet, but I couldn't wait much longer to give Raj the go-ahead signal—he'd warned they wouldn't be able to fly that many models for too long without a midair collision.

"Now!" I shouted dramatically, waving my free hand in a large clockwise motion, as if on the deck of an aircraft carrier. Raj and crew, with laser-like precision, maneuvered their whirring 'copters into position over the heads of our primary targets and, at my cue, started offloading the cargo. In a gooey, almost slo-mo fashion, the globs of glitter began their descent toward our unsuspecting victims. As the sticky, glittery gunk landed in their hair and glommed onto their clothing, the faces of Brian, Prince Harry, and several of their surrounding toadies morphed from derision into a hilariously unintentional reenactment of Munch's *The Scream*.

"We nailed 'em!" I shouted into Caleb's ear, as if he couldn't see for himself. "This is even better than I hoped!"

"Their expressions are priceless. You'd think a flock of pigeons just torpedoed them with bird shit!" he shouted back.

I turned to high-five Ariel, but she had disappeared into the crowd. Chad was also nowhere to be seen.

Brian and Prince Harry tried to sling off some of the goop, to little avail. Even though we couldn't hear them, we didn't need a lip reader to tell us what they were shouting. The crowd around them seemed highly amused by the whole thing. I got the sense they might have enjoyed seeing the "big men on campus" squirm as much as we did.

Once the glitter bombs had been dropped, I signaled Raj to begin one last flyover before we hoofed it back to the food court to await Eastern Prep's almost certain retaliation.

The helicopters arranged themselves in a V-formation and began the dramatic, choreographed finale we had practiced earlier. Instead of scattering to the four winds, the audience below looked up, mesmerized, perhaps wondering what fresh hell we were going to unleash next. At that moment, I looked up to see Ariel leaning over the side of the parapet of the floor above. She gave a thumbs up to someone in Teasers and I craned my head to see who it could be. I spotted Chad standing next to the deejay's turntable and wondered what was up.

Ariel disappeared for a moment and then reappeared, her hands mysteriously cradling something. She reached out and flung the contents into the flight path of the helicopters. Glue-free glitter fell in small tornadoes, whirling in the air as though magically tossed by a coterie of errant fairy godmothers. What was she doing? We didn't plan this. But it *was* breathtaking.

Though prepared for myriad responses to the earlier bombardment ranging anywhere from mild annoyance to outright anger, it would have taken Nostradamus to foresee what actually happened next. As the glitter fell like ticker tape onto upturned faces and outstretched arms, a pulsating beat began to pour from Teasers' speakers and out into the hallway. The volume was maxed so high you could no longer hear the helicopters whirring overhead, though they were just above arm's reach. The deejay was playing one of those inimitably danceable beats that you can't help but lean into, and rather than devolving into chaos, most people were smiling and spinning as if Ariel was dispensing laughing gas instead of glitter. Several of our crew rushed in to join the festivities, paying no heed whatsoever to my earlier words of warning. Caleb and I glanced at each other in disbelief. In addition to exacting unholy vengeance on Brian and his minions, thanks to our good fairy, Ariel, we'd apparently unleashed an epic rave. Everyone—well, almost everyone—had put their differences aside to share the newly minted dance floor. Brian and Prince Harry were nowhere to be seen, while Rachel and the Itneys appeared to be having a *telenovela*-style squabble in the far corner.

"Now what?" Caleb yelled into my ear.

"If you can't beat 'em, join 'em," I yelled back, leading him in the direction of the dance floor.

CHAPTER THIRTEEN

Unless I Be Reliev'd by Prayer

The combination of sweat, glitter, and endorphins was intoxicating as we joined a circle taking shape on the dance floor. At the center, Alfredo's slammin' pop-and-lock moves drew cheers and whistles from our erstwhile foes while Stacy Scott upped the ante with some crowd-inciting freestyle. Public school and private school kids intermingled as if we'd known each other since kindergarten and were now carousing together at our senior prom. Perhaps the United Nations could learn to resolve international conflicts with that great equalizer, the dance-off, I mused.

On the other side of the circle, I caught Ariel's face intermittently as she jumped up and down like a spastic terrier. My poor, "fun-sized" friend was attempting to peer over the rows of people crowded in front of her. I beckoned her to stand by me for a better view, but just then she was lifted up above the crowd in one fluid movement. A chivalrous Chad had hoisted her to a seated position on his right shoulder as if she weighed no more than a gallon of milk—which, truth be told, was probably the case. Thunderstruck, Ariel found my eyes in the crowd and stared at me with incredulity, silently mouthing, "Oh. My. God!"

"Happy Birthday!" I mouthed back at her, knowing that she'd be replaying this moment—and, perhaps, this whole night—in her head for a long time to come.

Meanwhile, I was again surprised that Caleb and I had somehow managed to find a happy medium with our movements on the dance floor. Certainly I'd had to temper some of my more intricate steps, but he wasn't nearly the clodhopper I'd expected him to be in spite of his accidentally treading on my toes a few times.

"Oh god—my bad!" he said after one such incident. "Are you alright?" He grabbed my shoulder with his free hand and brought his face close to mine so I could hear him through the din.

"Watch it, mister. I'm not the sort of person you can just walk all over," I said teasingly.

"*That* I know," he said with a grin. "Don't worry."

The music downshifted to something a bit slower, and a few people on the floor paired up as if to slow dance. Oh no. The deejay had been spot-on till now, but I suddenly found myself wishing a plague upon his house. Caleb and I were finally getting along okay, but that was a far cry from wanting to sway arm-in-arm with him to some cheesy light FM song. Besides, I had urgent business to attend to, and by business, I meant *business*.

I yanked Caleb in the direction of Ariel and Chad. The football star had gently placed my colleague back down on the ground and they were looking at each other a bit expectantly.

"Ariel, I need your help," I said, firmly.

"Wha—? *Now?*"

"Yes, *now.*"

"Are you sure it can't wait? I mean, I thought you said the copter run would be our last act of defiance!"

"Ariel, please, please, *please* come with Caleb and me. I need you! I wouldn't ask if it weren't important." My loyal friend sighed and gave Chad a sweet shrug, clearly hesitant to part ways with him but bound by what had become a sisterly allegiance to me.

"Well, thanks for the lift." She glanced at him and then averted her eyes in a blush.

"No problem, Tink." As he said this, Chad reached down and brushed a bit of purple glitter from Ariel's face with the palm of his hand. I hadn't the time to be sufficiently flabbergasted by this wholly unexpected kernel of romance I perceived between them. With Caleb and Ariel struggling to keep up, I shuffled as quickly as I could away from the party.

"So where are we going, your highness?" he asked.

"Believe me, you don't want to know." I grabbed a men's silk tie off an accessories kiosk en route. "We're going to need this."

***

Three people, one pair of handcuffs, and a three-by-five-foot bathroom stall; Harry Houdini couldn't have thought up a dicier tight spot for one of his great escapes, but here I was, finally attempting to soothe the savage beast—my bladder.

Caleb was standing with his face toward the stall door, blindfolded by the yellow-striped necktie so he couldn't see a thing. That, paired with the handcuffs and the grimace on his face, made him look like a hostage in the final hours of a long and intense negotiation for his release.

The embarrassment factor was excruciating in more ways than one. I'd wanted to turn on all the faucets in an attempt, I'd hoped, to keep Caleb from hearing the sound of me peeing. It seemed absurdly wrong to have any guy—let alone, this one—hear me tinkle. But alas, they were those automatic dealios that turn themselves off after ten seconds to save water. I'd hoped my chatterbox coworker would keep up her mile-a-minute play-by-play of the night long enough to drown out the sound.

Common girl knowledge the world over: Pulling down a pair of tights is hard enough with both hands, and virtually impossible with only one. So like an Elizabethan lady-in-waiting, Ariel dutifully stooped next to me, helping me shimmy my red tights and undies down past my knees. The skirt of my jumper hid the money shot, if you will, so even if Caleb had wanted to sneak a peek (and he didn't seem interested at the moment), he wouldn't have gotten to see much beyond the awkward visual of me hunched on the can. Ariel was wrestling with the protective seat cover made of tissue paper.

"It keeps slipping off the seat," she said. "I hate these stupid things!"

"Never mind! I'll crouch." I whispered this into her ear, just wanting the nightmare to conclude.

It was a tremendous relief to answer the now-insistent call of nature, but having held it in for so long, the process of elimination took mortifyingly longer than your average bathroom break. When it was clear that I'd finally emptied the kettle, so to speak, Ariel ripped off some toilet paper and handed it to me before we repeated the painstaking process of hiking my tights and unmentionables back north of the border.

"What are you guys doing back there, lacing up a corset?" Caleb said. "I thought girls took longer than guys in the bathroom because they were primping. I didn't realize a simple pee was an undertaking on par with sequencing the human genome."

I was about to respond but held my tongue when we heard the sound of the ladies' room door squeaking open. It was shame-inducing enough to have my bathroom break turn into a team sport, but to have someone find us crammed unnaturally together in the stall was enough to make all three of us clam up and assess the situation.

A cadre of high heels clomped across the marble floor accompanied by a garble of voices a few decibels higher than the roar of a jet engine. Ariel's face registered semi-panic.

"I canNOT. *Even.* Deal," Whitney said in a rage. "You do *not* do something like this to Whitney Elaine Emerson and live to tell—hiccup!—about it."

"Whatever, you're not the only victim here," Britney shot back. "C'mon, don't be a booze hog. Hand it to me." We heard the sound of liquid jostling in a glass bottle. "Uggh, this is rotgut. I'm not sure we should be drinking it straight."

"Like, what do you mean? It'd be safe if we were lesbians?"

After a confused pause, both girls erupted into inordinate peals of laughter until Britney abruptly halted midsnicker and added. "Seriously, couldn't you have at least added some, like, Apple Pucker to mask the turpentine taste?"

"Sorry, I'm not a freakin' 'mixologist'—you told me to swipe something that would get us shitfaced. Well, this stuff is the beverage of champions according to Nate's frat party postmortem e-mails. I'm already feeling a little bit cross-eyed, which proves this is hardcore hooch. Oh—speaking of Nate, we're, like, technically still together, so not a word to him about any of this mess."

I tried in vain to get a glimpse of the girls through a crack in the stall, failing to see why Whitney would be so worried that her college boyfriend hundreds of miles away would actually dump her over Ariel's little make-under. Not that I'd seen the results, but I didn't get the impression it was anything that a few weeks' time and a trip to a salon for some color corrections wouldn't fix.

"How could we not have seen it?" Britney leaned her back abruptly against our stall, rattling the door in the process. "I feel so stupid."

"And poor Rach," Whitney said. "You and I got played, sure, but she's the one who's hurting the most. I could see on her face how messed up she was. Her therapist's going to be, like, back at square one."

"This will *not* go unpunished," said Britney, clearly seething. "God, I need to be anesthetized. Give me another swig."

Wow. I knew my little bunny prank messed with Rachel's head, but it never occurred to me that it would be as serious as the Itneys were implying. It had just been a harmless joke, hadn't it? I glanced at Ariel, who looked as if she was a drug lord hiding out from the feds. If the Itneys were going this bitchcakes about the incidents we'd pulled earlier, I needed to run some interference for her sake. After all, they hopefully still had no idea that I was the puppetmaster who'd pulled Ariel's strings. I flashed my coworker the universal gesture for "Stay put!"—and reached past Caleb's right hip to unlock the stall door. Nudging him from behind, he and I stumbled out of the stall as if quite by accident, leaving Ariel behind.

I was about to feign surprise at seeing them, only I didn't have to. Seeing the number Ariel had done on them back at the salon made my jaw fly open. They both looked like they'd been hosed down with carrot juice, and their coiffes resembled frightful "mall hair" circa 1992. I tried my best to keep from staring at their depraved transformation, but needn't have worried. The Itneys were far too distracted by the shock of seeing yours truly—manacled to Caleb—stumbling out of a bathroom stall.

"What are *you* doing here?" they both said. I glanced guiltily at Caleb and rubbed my hand over my lips. Thankfully, he evinced his usual demeanor—stonefaced—and let me do all the talking.

"Sorry, girls. I guess we just got a little . . . worked up." (Desperate times called for desperate measures.)

"Really, Miranda? With *him*? And handcuffs? Ew. That's, like, totally gross."

The implied insult of Caleb rubbed me the wrong way. I was the only one allowed to express any feelings of repulsion for him, dammit! My defensive instincts kicked in.

"Wow, you guys look . . . *different*."

"Huh?" Britney said, as if completely unaware of how hideous she looked. "Oh, right. Your coworker—Ariel, is it?" I nodded.

"I mean, she'ssssweet girl and all," Britney said, tripping through her consonants, "but somebody really ought to tell her she's not cut out to work in the personal beauty industry. I wouldn't hire her to groom my dog."

"Yeah," Whitney said, nodding. "I don't know how long she's been in the trainee program at Blissworks, but, like, I think she needs a lot more practice. I mean, god help her first bikini wax client! It's a shame, because the poor thing seemed so passionate about it. I really hope she's got a Plan B. Maybe computers or something . . . she told us about some really cool app."

This wasn't adding up. A minute ago these two were foaming at the mouth about Ariel's pranks, but now they acted only mildly put-out by the whole experience. They frankly seemed oblivious that they'd even been the butt of any joke. As I mentally tried to work out what in the name of sweet baby Jesus was going on, Whitney changed the subject.

"Good to see there's life after Brian, at least," she said, pointing a limp arm in the direction of Caleb, whom, truth be told, we were all treating like a potted plant. "I mean, you've clearly moved on."

"Yeah . . . I guess all's well that ends well," I said with a shrug. I was certain they were setting me up for some scathing insult and considered preempting them with a caustic remark of my own. Instead, I opted to play it chill until I could figure out why they were being so uncharacteristically approachable. I'd heard of friendly drunks before, but I never imagined the Itneys would fall under that category.

"*Ends* swellll?!" Britney half-slurred and half-huffed. "Not for Brian, if I have any slay in the matter."

"You don't like him?" I asked. Now I was completely lost. "He's a total man whore."

I wasn't about to argue her point, cryptic as it was.

"But I swear, Brit" Whitney said, "I had no clue he was playing you, too. He promised me that he was ending things with Rachel as soon as all the dust had settled on the SAT crap—I took him at his word."

"Yeah, well he must have been working off a script, because he basically was feeding me those same freakin' lines," said her pal. "He didn't tell you that his love for you was, like, 'deep as the sea,' did he?"

"Oh, he is unbelievable. Yeah, I think it was 'boundless as the sea.' God, he probably ripped that off some hack on Google!" (Come to think of it, that line sounded vaguely familiar to me, too.) "I think I was just vulnerable, with Nate being away and all," Whitney said. "But it's inexcusable. I won't blame Rachel if she never speaks to me again."

"Don't beat yourself up, Whit. I feel guilty, too, but he was the one who had all three of us snowed."

"You mean, Brian was cheating on Rachel with *both* of you?" I said. "And neither of you knew?"

"Not until tonight," Whitney moped. "We, like, literally put two-and-two together—"

"It equals *four*. As in, two chicks too many. What would you call that, a love quadrangle?" Britney got lost in her drunken muse.

"Whatever," Whitney said. "Rachel is totally hulking out right now. God, the look on her face. And *you*," she looked at Britney before hurling herself emotionally into her arms. "You've got to know, girl, I would *NEVER* betray you like that! I mean, I know it looks like I would because I was basically doing it to Rachel and that makes me look like a backstabbing skank, but I never meant it that way. I love you like a sister—that's not just yearbook lip service!"

"It's okay, sweetie, I know. It wasn't our fault. I think there's a name for it. Like Sherlock Holmes syndrome or something. It's where you start believing all the bullshit that psychopaths tell you. I saw a show about it once on TV." She meant Stockholm Syndrome, and I'm pretty sure that she was way off base using it to describe their situation, but whatever. Britney was sobbing now, too, and I chalked up this exaggerated three-hankie display to the fact that they were by now fairly blitzed.

"No guy should ever cost us our friendship," Whitney said. "I mean, we've known each other, like, forevs. We can't let some total asshat drive a wedge between us. God, I can't wait to see how he tries to backpedal through this shit storm when we bust him on it."

"He's not even that cute."

"No kidding. I always thought he resembled one of those Mexican hairless dogs."

Caleb leaned in to me during their tirade and whispered, "Is this what people mean by righteous indignation?"

Smirking, I motioned for him to hush up. I found myself more fascinated by the Itneys' evaluation of their plight than empathetic. Each of them had gladly adopted the mantle of "the other woman" when he'd offered them the chance. True, their opinion of Brian as a regular rat bastard got no qualms from me. But they were the ones stupid enough to fall for him and his bogus charms! Okay, maybe I fell for those charms, too, but I didn't know he was the cheating type, and it behooved him to stay on my good side while he was turning my little side business into the scam of the century. My rose-colored glasses had been smashed weeks ago as far as that was concerned. Damn, it wasn't easy to be the outsider looking in on the demimonde I once thoughtlessly inhabited. And seeing it through Caleb and Ariel's eyes—that was even worse.

The bathroom door swung open again, and in walked Rachel, flush-faced with black rivulets of melted mascara tears on her cheeks. The second she saw us, she spun on her heel and tried to scurry back through the still-open door, but the Itneys each grabbed her by one elbow and hauled her back in.

"Rachel, don't leave," Whitney said "Give us a chance to explain!"

"What's to explain? That you stole my boyfriend?"

"Rach, it definitely wasn't like that."

"Yeah, well, my apologies for not believing a word you lying bitches have to say." She glanced at me. "What's with Princess Leia and the Wookie?"

"Shhh. . . ." Britney said in a loud whisper, "It's Miranda's NEWWWW LOVAHHH."

"He's not exactly—" I protested, elbowing a smirking Caleb before deciding there was no point in clarifying our relationship.

"C'mon, Rach, are we really going to let a man, like, come between us? Even one as rich and popular as Brian?" Whitney asked.

"You're damp shtraight we won't! Shisterhood. That's what I'm talking about."

"Britney, you're drunk."

"Am not—"

"And, Whitney, you must be high if you think I'm going to just forgive and forget. Newsflash: Without me, you two are going to be about as popular as Miss Tube Steak USA here."

"Shut it. I would *never*—no offense, Miranda—work in food service, especially not a freakin' hot dog stand."

"Or wear primary-colored polyeshter!"

"That's not the point. You're going to be so friendless, you'll wish you worked at Hot-Dog Kabob. One word from me and you two are social pariahs. And just try to keep me quiet."

"Why do you always have to be such a bitch?" Whitney said.

"You might as well enroll in public school tomorrow and get it over with!"

I'd been soaking up this train wreck triumvirate with a combination of detached amusement and growing annoyance. Clearly I wasn't the only one, because Caleb finally cleared his throat to bring Rachel and the Itneys' shouting match to a halt.

"I'm an innocent bystander here, but I gotta ask something." All four of us looked at him expectantly. "Rachel, right?" Rachel nodded. "Didn't you do the same thing to Miranda that," he pointed to the Itneys, "those two did to you?"

"Yep," Whitney said, nodding overeagerly. "She did."

"Uh huh," Britney said, before hiccuping.

"So," Rachel said with a shrug.

"So, you really don't have much 'victim' cred on this one. What goes around, comes around. My recommendation? Forgive them or you're screwed, karmically speaking." Caleb was giving off this total wiseman vibe, like he'd just exited the sacred confines of a Buddhist ashram. Rachel looked thoughtful.

"I suppose Sasquatch has a point. The person we should really be mad at is Brian. He is a flaming ball of poo. An emotional terrorist."

"Yeah, he basically, like, threw a dirty bomb at our friendship."

"That bashtard."

"Don't get me wrong—what you guys did was really not cool," Rachel said. "But let's go ahead and chalk it up to the fact that you were both probably jealous of me, in which case I forgive you. Besides, you're both drunk and look like roadkill right now. I imagine we've probably all been through enough today."

"Aw, really? I always knew you were the bigger person!" Instead of picking up on Britney's thinly veiled insult (even I couldn't tell if it had been deliberate or not), Rachel embraced her in a tight squeeze. Not one to be outdone, Whitney glommed on, too.

"Love you, guys."

"Love you more." Their meeting of the Mutual Adoration Society had officially commenced. Caleb looked flabbergasted by it all, but I was unfazed, having witnessed their love-hate histrionics plenty of times in the past.

"Brian is going to be wishing he wore ironclad boxers tonight," Rachel said, breaking free from the hug huddle and reaching for Britney's flask, "because it's time for us to go collectively rip him a new one."

"First we've got to find him," Whitney pointed out. "I didn't see him at the poor man's prom out there."

"He took off with Prince Harry to go get the glue off. Their eyelids were starting to stick shut," Britney said. "He told me if I met him down at Lane's Diamonds later we could do some window shopping. Claimed he needed hints for my birthday present next month, 'tho I think he was just angling to hook up."

"Perfect. Let's go corner and verbally fillet that bastard." Rachel turned to me uncertainly. "Do you wanna come?" Perhaps she was trying to extend the olive branch, or maybe she was just hoping I might do the heavy lifting for them and take charge, the way I always used to. Either way, it dawned on me that wasting one more second on my ex no longer sounded like a productive way to pass the time.

"You go ahead," I said with all the *bonhomie* I could muster. "It's really not my battle anymore."

CHAPTER FOURTEEN

A Thousand Twangling Instruments Will Hum about Mine Ears

While we'd been holed up in the ladies' room, the impromptu dance party had apparently ground to a halt as quickly as it began, leaving as its detritus shoe prints of gluey glitter, the lingering scent of sweaty bodies, and Chad, who appeared about as energized as a basset hound on a hot afternoon. A look of consternation flitted over Ariel's winsome features. I'd selfishly interrupted what could have been the penultimate moment of her teenage years. Although I knew she didn't bear me any ill will, I was even more determined after our recent time in the trenches to see her through the waning hours of her birthday. This had been a wild night; why not end it on an even crazier note? It was time to come out of my self-imposed retirement in order to orchestrate one more incredible feat. Only this time my coercive prowess would be for something far nobler than vengeance; this time it would be for love.

"Okay, guys," I said to my weary compatriots. "Move your gams—we're going on a shopping spree."

"Not on your life," said Caleb. "That's the absolute worst idea you've had all night. And that's saying something."

"Calm down, Dr. Killjoy." I pulled his arm encouragingly. "See where we're going first before you unleash your hissy fit on the world."

"I think we should go back to the food court and wait it out," Chad said.

"Overruled, counselor. No way. It's still Ariel's birthday. C'mon, we have to rally. We can rest when we're old."

"But where *are* we going?" Ariel asked with a resigned expression.

"Doesn't anybody trust me?" I said, pretending to be offended.

"You know she won't stop bullying us until we go with her, right?" Chad said to Caleb.

"I guess so. She'll pull me along like an obstinate mule if I object, so I might as well do it the easy way." He gave an exaggerated sigh.

"Your enthusiasm is simply overwhelming," I said to him, throwing a grateful smile over my shoulder at Chad. I remembered my first conversation with the jock earlier in the evening and couldn't believe how wrong I'd pegged him. He was a total sweetheart.

I commandeered Raj and another mall employee, Seth, to join us, but refused to give any indication of where, exactly, we were going.

After catching the elevator to the second floor and hanging a right at the mall's central intersection, there we were, standing like weary pilgrims outside the gates of Mecca. I glanced at Chad and Caleb who stared in catatonic rapture as if listening to a chorus of heavenly angels. I could only hope they didn't start drooling.

"The Guitar Center," Ariel said, quite unnecessarily as the sign loomed large above our heads. "But I thought we were going shopping."

"Exactly. Can you roll up the gate, Seth?" With tousled shoulder-length hair and a Kurt Cobain slouch, Seth was a frequent visitor to Hot-Dog Kabob, as he suffered from what seemed to be an interminable case of "the munchies." He was also, incidentally, a sales clerk at this rock-lovers' Valhalla. Eternally grateful to me for being his alibi a few weeks ago when he turned up thirty-five minutes late to work (I'd sworn he was helping me change a flat tire . . . all my idea, of course), I hadn't chosen him to accompany our little assemblage by accident.

"So here's the thing," I said as we entered the store, "I think you guys should do your show."

"What do you mean?" Caleb said. "Here in the store? Not to be a jackass or anything, but this would be our smallest audience. Like, ever."

"No, not here, wise guy. In the food court. For everyone."

"Oh man, that could be cool," Seth said. "Like U2 performing 'Where the Streets Have No Name' on top of that building in downtown LA."

"*Cool?*" Ariel's eyes widened. "It will be like our very own Woodstock!"

"But we don't have Jake," Chad said from behind a drum set.

"I play bass," Seth said, picking one off the wall display and strumming it for emphasis. "I'm no Jake, but I know all your tunes. I'm a huge Butlers fan."

Chad looked expectantly at Caleb.

"Why not?" he said. "We don't have anything better to do." Caleb had by this point reached down to pick up a guitar from its stand on the floor.

"I've been hearing that excuse all night," he said absently, gazing awestruck at the instrument as if it might unlock the secrets of the universe. "We've got the equipment, but I don't know. . . ."

It was around this time that I realized there was one teensy, tiny flaw in my otherwise brilliant plan. If The Drunk Butlers played show in the food court, I'd have to be on stage with them. And not just jangling a tambourine or answering the call for more cowbell. No matter how legendarily talented he supposedly was, even Caleb couldn't play a guitar with only one hand.

"It's okay," I said anticipating Caleb's argument. "You'll just have to strum with my arm attached. I can keep up. You won't even notice I'm there."

"Riiighht. Because you're such a 'blend into the woodwork' kind of girl. Well, if we don't want to look like utter fools, we'd better start practicing." Ariel let out an exuberant squeal. "And, for the record," Caleb said, "I'm only doing this for the half-pint here, as a birthday favor. Not because I think it's a good idea."

"Noted. But first things first, Clapton. Let's get the ball rolling as far as setup. We'll just have to find a spare minute here and there to practice while we oversee everything."

Getting the food court prepped for a live performance was no mean feat. While Ariel spread the word at both ends of the mall that the show would begin in an hour's time, I deputized Raj and his crew as our official roadies. They obviously had the necessary techie credentials to set up the lighting and amps and, needless to say, they were thrilled to be tackling a project with such an obvious cool quotient for a change. Even Caleb finally seemed to be jonesing on the idea, overseeing soundchecks and scribbling out a playlist for the guys. *My* outward enthusiasm, on the other hand, belied inner turmoil. Soon I'd be on stage in front of an audience that was sure to include the classmates who'd been my nemeses of late. What if people started heckling me again like they had at the start of my shift? What if I couldn't keep up with Caleb's playing and made a complete ass of myself? The chances of both those scenarios happening simultaneously seemed high.

Grady was milling about, trying to offer some assistance but frankly just getting in the way. Major butterflies were accumulating in my stomach and I wondered if maybe the mall cop could grant me a last-minute reprieve.

"You busy, Grady?" I asked.

"Just ascertaining that everything's under control down here," he replied.

"As a matter of fact, it's not. I'm fully freaking out right now. Do I look like the fifth Beatle?"

"I'm not sure I know what that means, but no, I reckon you don't."

"Exactly. Which means I've got to get out of these shackles. Like, *yesterday.* Can't you go see if you can find a pair of bolt cutters, or *anything* that might work?"

He cracked his knuckles, intentionally, seeming to ruminate on my request.

"Well, I'm not sure I'll be able to find anything that'll do the trick—like I said before, they're steel alloy—but I guess I can go try to dig something up."

"Once again, you're my hero!" I hugged Grady, tangling an unprepared Caleb up in the embrace. "Just do it fast. We don't have much longer!"

Caleb and Raj were engaged in a heated discussion about an amp issue when Ariel flitted over to whisper in my ear, "You're going to be great."

"Remind me why I'm doing this again?" I whispered back.

"For your real friends, of course: Me, Caleb, and Chad."

"That's sweet of you to say, but I'm not sure we're *all* friends. Mr. Darcy over here," I indicated Caleb with a nod, "finds me barely tolerable."

"You just got off on the wrong foot."

"Well, circumstances *have* been less than favorable," I admitted. "But anyway, I might get off the hook if Grady gets back in time."

"Never mind. Just go have fun," said Ariel. "I don't get the impression you've gotten to do that much lately."

***

Thanks to the lighting, the food court was beginning to feel more like a cool underground club than the abysmal hell hole it usually was. The crowd grew steadily and the anticipatory buzz in the room was electric. Ariel and some of the other kids were handing out free sodas and 'dogs while Chase, the deejay from Teasers, opened the show with a set that sampled popular Drunk Butler tunes. To create our "stage," the crew had removed potted palm trees and relocated "The Mariner," a rustic, life-sized fishing boat that normally stood as a decorative fixture on a raised platform in the center of the food court. Caleb, Chad, Seth, and I were "backstage," warming up in the back room of Hot-Dog Kabob.

"Seth, just follow our lead," Caleb said. "Don't forget there's a second bridge in 'Fathom Five.' Miranda, you okay?"

"Sure, I'm fine."

"You don't look fine," Chad said.

"Don't remind me. It's my fifteen minutes of fame, and I don't even have my makeup kit. I was at least hoping to offset this dorky uniform with a smoky eye or something."

"No, you *look* great. But, I mean, you also kind of look like you're going to be sick."

"Someone get a bucket," Seth yelled. "We've got a spewer!"

"Not necessary," I said, rolling my eyes. "Like I said, I'm fine." Though at that moment I was really wishing I'd eaten something more substantial than a corn dog.

"It's just stage fright," Caleb said, putting his hand on my shoulder. "We all get it."

"*You* don't look nervous." I glanced up at him. He looked the same as he had all night, so unfairly above it all.

"I just learned how to channel it," Caleb said. "Ask Chad."

"He's a basket case inside," Chad confirmed. "The first three shows we did, the opening band had to do a double encore because he was. . . ."

"Go ahead. You can tell her."

"Worshipping the porcelain gods. Profusely."

"Gross," I said. "Like I needed that visual. But it does make me feel better. Thanks."

"Just stick with me—as if you had any choice," Caleb said, chuckling. "You'll be fine. But for once, you're not allowed to be in control. Think of your arm as a wet noodle, and I'll take care of the strumming.

"Wet noodle?"

"Try to keep your elbow away from the strings if you can, but if you stiffen up we're screwed. Oh—and like it or not, I'm going to need you to stand as close to me as possible. Think barnacle."

Five minutes later, we were onstage, though I don't remember how we got there, and Caleb was belting out the first tune, "So Long Lives This." I'm sure I looked like a proverbial deer in headlights, but my eyes hadn't adjusted yet and I couldn't see a thing.

My ears worked just fine, however, and let me tell you— boy could he sing! In front of his audience, Caleb completely opened up. No longer the curmudgeon I was familiar with, he was downright charismatic. I may have been in the thick of the action, but I quickly forgot about all the eyeballs that were upon me and just let myself enjoy the show along with the rest of the crowd swaying in front of me, some of them waving their softly glowing cell phones aloft in the darkness. It wasn't hard to follow Caleb's instructions about just letting go; the music was both lilting and intense. With just three instruments, they managed to sound otherworldly, as if sweeping their listeners upon the crest of a rhythmic tidal wave that crescendoed into a realm both desolate and familiar. I'd already heard a smattering of the songs a few times on the radio, but now I had the luxury of being able to really comprehend the lyrics as Caleb belted them out with a deep-but-plaintive voice. The pervading themes were of love and of loneliness, disenchantment and heartache; a paean to powers greater than us and anthems for futures unknown. It struck a chord—not just with me, I was certain, but with every other adolescent out there bobbing his or her head solemnly to the music. As I nestled against his side to give him the leeway he needed to play his instrument, I almost couldn't believe that my verbally stingy adjunct was this poetic. What's more, the way his black hair fell upon his steel-gray eyes as he leaned over the mic stand, I couldn't help but think he bore an ever-so-slight resemblance to one Johnny Depp. I would never admit as much to him, of course, and I was semi-irritated at myself for even thinking it. But this was proof positive: a simple guitar slung over a guy's torso can transform even the most feral-looking dude into someone, well, kind of *hot*. I was embarrassed to feel a twinge of jealousy over the groupies pressed against the raised-platform stage, staring up at Caleb as they mouthed the words to the chorus.

"Okay, guys, thanks for obliging our brief attempts at soul-searching," he said after the conclusion of "Tell No Tales."

"Play 'Free Bird!'" Dex's voice boomed mockingly from the audience. He was sitting on a plastic chair, his leg elevated on another with a bag of ice over his swollen ankle.

"No way, man," Caleb answered. "It's time to lighten the mood." Still leaning over the microphone, he pivoted his head and smiled coyly at Chad who was seated at the drum set behind him. "Someone turned seventeen tonight, and that's cause enough to rip it up a little bit." He turned his face to mine and gave a saucy wink that caught me off guard. "Don't think for a second the Butlers don't know how to ROCK. YOUR. WORLD."

The crowd went nuts, of course, and Chad tapped his drumsticks together over his head in a four-time beat as their signal to launch into the next song, the same jaunty little tune I'd been jamming to in the mall parking lot earlier. The pace of Caleb's playing had sped up and then some, but I didn't care. I let him bandy my arm about frenetically as he strummed away, and I allowed my head do the same, tossing it from side-to-side. As my hair hit my face in staccato bursts, I felt liberated—and happy. Not since the SAT bust went down more than a month ago had I experienced anything even remotely close to this feeling. Come to think of it, it'd been a long time even before that. I felt like the real me had been in a deep freeze but was finally thawing out. Ironically, it had taken the coldest blizzard on record to make it happen.

We'd just begun another punchy pop tune when the sound of high-pitched caterwauling brought the musicians to a full stop. What sounded at first like the Charge of the Light Brigade was, in fact, the familiar clop-trot of high-heeled boots. Britney rounded the corner near the food court at a fast clip screaming for help, followed by Brian, with Rachel and Whitney close behind. As Caleb silenced the band, my onetime cronies approached the stage. I gasped when I saw my ex, whose face and right hand were both bleeding. Wow, I knew the girls were pissed, but "assault-and-battery" pissed? I didn't think they had it in them.

"What the hell did you guys do to him?" I said.

"We?!" Rachel said, trying to catch her breath! "Jeez, we're not from Jersey!"

"We found him at Lane's Diamonds," Whitney said. "Someone smashed through the display cases and wiped out most of the bling."

The news of the incident elicited gasps from the crowd as people drew nearer to get the low-down. We'd all pretty much figured the computer thief had long since left the premises, but Brian's face indicated otherwise.

"I walked in on him shoving strands of diamonds and pearls into a garbage bag, like it was pirate booty," Brian stammered, clearly spooked. "I guess he panicked, because he ran off with the loot. The girls showed up just a few seconds later."

"Oh my god, Brian, are you okay?!" I may have loathed him, but not enough to derive pleasure from his ordeal. "Did he attack you?"

"Oh, this?" he glanced at his bleeding hand. "No. I tried to run after the guy but I slipped and did a faceplant on the broken glass all over the floor."

"Wait—you saw the thief?" Caleb asked. Brian nodded.

"Yes and no. The lights in the store were all off, and he was wearing a black ski mask and a heavy black coat. He also had a pretty serious firearm." I instantly remembered my manager, Randall, skipping out early. He'd been well-armed for the weather—but had he also been *armed*-armed?

"This is beyond ballsy." Caleb folded his arms, forgetting momentarily that I was still attached. He dropped his hands by his side, letting mine fall with a thud alongside his. "And yet it doesn't make any sense. It's an ideal day for a klepto, I get it; but where's the guy hiding out? Where's he offloading the loot? We're all locked in the building right now, and even if he was able to make a break for it, he'd leave a literal trail of evidence in the snow . . . if he didn't freeze to death in the elements."

"It's gotta be an inside job," I said, eyeing Brian. His hair stuck straight up from trying to get the glue out, and there was glitter stuck to his eyelashes. The bright red blood now smeared across his lips made him look a little like Ziggy Stardust, oddly enough.

"Someone go find Grady," said a voice toward the back of the crowd. I remembered having sent him on my selfish errand for bolt cutters and felt guilty that he wasn't here to do his real job now that we needed him.

"As if Mighty Mouse could do anything?" Quinn said. "There's a homicidal maniac among us and he hasn't done bupkiss to try to find Mike. I'm worried, you guys! I think Mike could be in serious trouble!"

Or, he could be the one behind all the trouble, I thought without voicing my suspicion aloud.

CHAPTER FIFTEEN

You Cram These Words Into Mine Ears Against the Stomach of My Sense

Chad patched up Brian's face as best he could using the Band-Aids from our antediluvian first aid kit. The excitement triggered by his run-in with the thief was starting to dissipate, but no one felt much in the mood for more music in light of the recent developments. Grady had returned to let me know his search for cuff cutters had been fruitless. I'm not sure what bummed out the bumbling security guard more: realizing he'd been at the wrong end of the mall to catch the perp red-handed, or finding out we'd already "debriefed" Brian on all the pertinent details.

"Maybe we could work up a police sketch of the guy," he naively suggested, desperately trying to assert his authority in some official capacity. "Do we have any budding artists?"

"Yeah, nimrod. Because only the next Picasso could differentiate between the subtle nuances of a wool ski cap versus a cotton/Lycra blend." Rachel's attitude toward the minimum-wage employee was unduly cruel. It didn't seem fair to pick the low-hanging fruit, socially speaking.

With his free hand, Caleb closed the lid on a guitar case and flipped the latches shut while Seth and the roadies started rolling amps back in the direction of The Guitar Center. Chad came over to hand us each a bottle of water, Ariel gamely skipping to keep up with his long strides.

"That was *awesomesauce!*" she declared. "You guys were amazing! You, too, Miranda."

"Yeah, right. Do they give out Grammys for 'Best Pointless Nonentity Randomly Up On Stage?' Because I'd at least get the write-in vote. But she's right, you were both pretty incredible," I said, staring at Caleb directly.

"Thanks. I'm pretty sure that was a rock-n-roll first," he answered. "And don't be so modest. You were a champ up there.

I heard you chiming in on that last song, too. Your voice is pretty decent."

"You think?"

"I think."

"Well, anyway," I said, flustered. "That was mind-blowing. I'm pretty sure we all needed something like that tonight. It's been . . . something."

"Noooooo kidding."

While Ariel helped Chad take down the drum set, I grabbed the case for the bass so Caleb and I could walk both guitars back to the music store.

"Is that too heavy for you?" he asked, as we headed upstairs.

"No, I got it. But thanks. Good thing you're not the type of rocker who smashes the guitar onstage," I said with a laugh. "You break it, you buy it."

"I tried to be gentle. Thanks again. That was pretty cool."

"I just had the idea. You're the one with the actual talent."

"Yeah, well, don't sell yourself short."

After returning the guitars no worse for wear, we were about to hop the down escalator back to the food court when Caleb instead grabbed my hand and steered me into the Got Games store.

"Why are we stopping here?" My heartbeat kicked into gear for some strange reason as he led me through the empty, darkened store to the register. "Don't tell me you're planning to check the weather forecast on your trusty Magic Eight Ball," I said.

"Nah. It's just a little detour. There's something I wanted you to have." He reached under the counter and retrieved a cellophane-wrapped flat rectangular box. "Here."

"The *Avalanche X* game," I said. "You had a copy?"

"Yeah. We keep one on hand, on the down-low, in case some V.I.P. comes in looking for it."

"But I'm not a V.I.P."

"Says who? I've been chained to you all night, and from what I've seen, you are . . . well," he cleared his throat, "you're clearly someone special. You acted like getting your hands on this game was important, and if you say it is, then I trust you."

"Gosh. I don't know what to say other than, thank you. It's definitely going toward a good cause. I mean, I don't want you to think it was just something I wanted for myself."

"That's pretty evident. I wouldn't mistake you for a gamer. Besides, you may be infuriatingly stubborn and a born meddler, but I can tell your heart's definitely in the right place."

Before I could respond, we heard a shuffling sound coming from behind a display on the other side of the darkened store. I instantly remembered the thief, and Caleb must have been thinking the same thing. He put his finger to his lips and grabbed one of those video game baseball bats, which looked hollow and flimsy. Keeping me safely behind him, Caleb silently inched forward to where the sound of the noise had come from. He peered around the corner of the display while I waited with sweaty palms, knowing a one-handed swipe with a fake plastic baseball bat didn't stand a chance against some nut job with a gun.

While I prepared myself to scream bloody murder and aim a swift kick at the felon's family jewels, Caleb placed the bat on the floor, then glanced back and gestured for me to check it out. Huh? I inched forward. Curled up, sound asleep on the store's threadbare carpet was none other than my glitter-bestrewn former flame.

"Brian!!!???" My shriek woke him with a frightened start.

"Wha—?!!! Miranda!" He rolled out of his fetal position and got to his feet, still groggy-eyed and confused.

"What are *you* doing here?"

"I guess I fell asleep. I wandered off to get away from all the drama."

"What do you mean?"

"Well, I'm about as welcome in your food court as parents at prom."

"So. I thought you were dictator down at your end of the mall?"

"Yeah, but they all revolted and came down this way. Meanwhile, Rachel and the girls want my head on a stake."

"Ah yes, the downside of having multiple girlfriends."

"They aren't my girlfriends."

"Harem, hootchie mamas . . . call them what you will. We talked to them earlier." I gestured to Caleb. "They were steamed."

"I don't know what they told you," Brian said, scratching the back of his neck, "but I made it pretty clear to all three of them where my head was at. They knew I wasn't interested in a relationship. It was a friends-with-benefits sort of thing. I assumed they were all in the loop. I mean, that's all you chicks do is gossip about stuff like that."

"That's an interesting take."

"Why would I want to get into something heavy a month after you dumped me?" he said.

"Come again?"

"You broke my heart, Miranda!"

Had I been socked in the face with a frozen turkey, I couldn't have been more stunned.

"What . . . the HELL . . . are you talking about? I took the fall for your asinine cheating scam! You LIED. You accused me of orchestrating it! Then you topped it all off by carrying on with my best friend, and you've been treating me like pond scum ever since!"

"Is that really what you think?" Brian said, looking aghast.

"It's not what I think. It's what actually happened."

"I know it was wrong to have singled you out about the SATs, and believe me, it killed me to have to do it. But here's the thing: You didn't have anything to do with the cheating, so I knew you couldn't actually get busted. At least not in a legal sense."

"Oh, nice. As if that explains everything?"

"Look, I was certain there'd be no case against you, and I figured you wouldn't get hurt. I mean, you're Miranda Prospero, 'the Teflon teen.' When have you not been able to land butter-side up in the world?"

"Yeah, well, I was toast, all right."

"I know, and I'm so sorry about that. I never figured the school board would come down so hard on you, but that's nothing compared to what I would have been facing had I not 'named names.' I wanted to try to explain all that to you at the time," he continued, "but as part of the deal they'd instructed me not to speak with you. That day of the meeting with our parents, I could tell from the look on your face that you'd never forgive me. You can't even begin to fathom how that wrecked me."

"But I. . . ." I tried to jump in, to no avail.

"Crap, Miranda, I was in *love* with you. I still am." The room got eerily quiet. Caleb had wisely chosen to remain silent as my conversation continued.

"What about Rachel? Britney? Whitney? Am I missing anyone?"

"No. I don't know. I guess they're the 'cleanup' crew. They saw how much I was hurting and they were pretty overt about wanting to help me through it—with no strings attached. I mean, hell, they all three have boyfriends in college! As far as I was concerned, I thought we were just having a little fun. Apparently, they saw it differently."

"Apparently."

"I guess maybe I just don't understand chicks that way. But you weren't just some casual thing for me. You've got to know that. I mean, I'd do anything to turn back the clock and have you back in my life."

"But you've been so cruel to me! I don't understand any of this!"

"It was just stupid pride. I'm a guy; that's what we do when we're hurt. We try to hurt back. But I didn't mean any of it. What I said to your friend, the 'manic pixie girl,' was totally uncalled for, too. I need to apologize to her for that, I know. I just let Rachel and the girls egg me on. Tell me what I need to do, and I'll make it up to you!"

He spoke all the words I'd been wanting to hear, and yet, as they filtered through my brain they felt, at once, both consoling and slippery. In the past month, he had shown me exactly the kind of man he was, but now here he was, changing his colors quicker than a chameleon in a Crayola factory. For weeks, I'd been wishing I could see him crawl through broken glass to make his way back to me, and to tell me this was all some giant mistake. Now, practically speaking, that's basically what he was doing, and my thoughts were all slamming into one another trying to sort out a response.

Despite my best efforts at keeping my shit together, the dam broke. I started to cry. These last few weeks had been so exhaustively painful for me, and I felt like I was reliving it all. My heart literally felt pierced; a shooting pain radiated up into my tightened throat as I breathed in uncontrollable little shudders. I instinctively reached my left hand up to wipe away the tears, inadvertently dragging Caleb's hand with it. Brian brushed my mangy bangs out of my eyes and tried to console me.

"Don't be sad," he whispered. "I'm so sorry I hurt you. Please let me try to fix it." I avoided his gaze, staring instead at a stack of classic board games on a lower shelf. When you really thought about it, the world was really just one giant board game on which we were mere pawns, subject always to a roll of the dice, or so it seemed. I eyed the titles on the boxes: *Chutes and Ladders . . . Trouble . . . The Game of Life . . . Mousetrap.* There were always going to be winners and losers, and one thing I knew about the human existence is that it basically boiled down to a series of calculated moves. I wondered, at this moment, if I was about to make the right one.

I allowed myself to imagine what it would be like if I let Brian back into my life. My worries would presumably vanish in an instant. With his rich-as-sin background, he'd take care of my debt and, best of all, I would no longer be Eastern Prep's resident pariah. A phoenix rising from the depths of the food court to become ruling snow bunny and shopaholic once again. Ignoring Caleb entirely, I glanced back up at Brian and eked out a small smile amid my sniffles.

"I've missed you so much," I choked through my tears. "I'm still really confused, and we're going to need a lot of time to rebuild and start over. But believe me when I say my life hasn't been the same without you in it."

Brian grabbed my face in both his hands and laid a small, tender kiss on my lips. I couldn't bring myself to glance in Caleb's direction, but we were in close enough proximity that I could hear the air escaping through his lips as if whispering to me his disappointment. I knew I was making the right decision, and yet

I wanted so badly to offer him an explanation, to tell him why I needed to see things through with my ex. But not here. Not now. In time, hopefully I could reassure him that the Miranda he'd come to know and, well, at least *like* over the course of this night hadn't changed. Had it?

"Talk about awkward," Brian said, looking over at Caleb (at least one of us had the courage to). "Three is *most definitely* a crowd. What's the story behind the handcuffs, anyway?"

"Stupid, really. Don't ask." I said. "We don't have the key, obviously."

"I'm going to go hit up the maintenance department and see if I can find something to break the lock or saw through those. I'll meet you back at the food court." He grabbed my free hand and squeezed it. "We can talk more freely then."

Caleb didn't say a word as he and I left Got Games and headed back toward the food court. I was speechless with embarrassment about the drama he'd witnessed with Brian and still couldn't bring myself to make eye contact with him. The silence between us was agonizing, but I preferred it, frankly, to anything he might have to say to me. I knew what he must be thinking, and no matter how justified I felt in my own heart, I didn't want to be one of "those girls" in his eyes. Though feeling uncharacteristically sheepish, I broke our silence when, out of my peripheral vision, I saw someone stumble out of the hallway that led from the janitorial staff's locker room.

"Oh my god," I said, stopping short. "It's Mike!" Deathly pale, the missing Treasure Hunt employee lurched toward us like a Spanish galleon bucking its way through a storm. Caleb rushed forward, dragging me along with him. We reached Mike just in time to catch him as he lost consciousness.

"Hey, Mike! Buddy, are you okay?" Caleb said. Crouching on the floor next to him, he pushed aside a piece of frayed rope to take Mike's pulse. A nasty gash on his forehead puckered with dried blood.

"He's not—" My hands flew to my mouth.

Caleb shook his head and, snapping his fingers in front of Mike's face, called out to him again. He blinked and opened his eyes. Groaning, he reached up to touch his forehead.

"Ow. . . ." he winced.

"That looks pretty bad. What happened?"

"I was in the back of the store polishing some antique silver we'd just got in." He tried to sit up, and we helped him scoot over so he could lean against the wall. "A dude wearing a ski mask came in through the back entrance brandishing a gun. I don't know, I guess we scuffled. Next thing I knew, I woke up in the janitor's locker room, duct tape over my mouth and tied to a chair. Finally managed to shred my way through the ropes with the corner of a desk . . . it took hours. I tried to call the cops, but the phone isn't working in there."

His brow furrowed in confusion, he looked back and forth between us. "What are you two still doing in the mall? It's the middle of the night."

"Just relax for a sec," Caleb said. "We'll catch you up on everything, but I want to make sure you're okay first."

"I'm fine, really. Just tell me what the hell's going on," he said, rubbing the raw marks on his wrist.

We sat down and filled him in on most of what had happened over the last few hours—the relevant stuff anyway.

"We should get him down to the food court," Caleb said to me. "Chad can take a look at his forehead."

"Quinn's there, too," I said. "She's been worried sick about you."

"Guys!" Appearing at the top of the escalator, Grady's face gave way to alarm when he saw us.

"Don't worry, he's okay," I said. "He had a run-in with the thief. Too bad he didn't get a glimpse of the guy's face." Once he realized Mike wasn't gravely injured, Grady excitedly referred to the incident as a "10-53," and we gave him the digest version of Mike's assault. I saw Seth materialize at the top of the escalator, and he dashed over when he saw us.

"And you can't remember anything else about the guy who did this?" he said after we'd filled him in.

"No, dude. I completely blacked out after he clocked me."

"This is why I've been asking you kids to quit wandering off," Grady said. "Miranda, you and I have always had an understanding with one another, but I'm afraid I'm going to have to pull rank and insist that you return to the food court, ASAP. And stay there, this time."

"We wouldn't have found Mike if we hadn't been up here," I said.

"No, Grady makes a good point," Caleb said. "Whoever's doing this is dangerous and unpredictable. Let's just go back and hunker down."

"Glad to see someone appreciates the seriousness of the situation," Grady said. "You guys will all be just fine if you stick together in one place."

"Come on, Miranda, let's just get back to base camp." Caleb's tone sounded almost defeatist. "But where's. . .? Aww, hell," he said. "I left my wallet back on the Got Games counter."

"No, you—" I started. He hadn't touched his wallet all night.

"Yes, yes I *did*," he said. "Grady, we're just going to run right back—give us two seconds. I know exactly where I left it. Can you guys help Mike down the escalator?"

Grady hesitated. "I was on my way down to the other end of the mall to convince the kids there to relocate to the food court. Strength in numbers, you know."

"I'll get Mike back," Seth said.

"Thanks, man," said Caleb. "We'll be back in a jiffy."

"See that you are," said Grady, turning on his heel to depart. With a backward glance, he added, "Don't let Miranda coerce you into any more detours!"

"No way," Caleb said. "She and I are through—with all that, I mean. Besides, I think Miranda has other priorities. We'll meet you back downstairs."

I waved at Mike as he disappeared down the escalator with Seth and then turned to Caleb, flummoxed.

"Why did you lie to him?"

"Because I'm not willing to be trapped in here like sitting ducks any more," he said. "This isn't just some petty crime. People are getting hurt, we haven't seen your friend Colin in hours. . . . This just doesn't smell right. We need the real police here—not McGruff the Crime Dog."

"Agreed, but what's your idea?"

"They stock ham radios at Radio Hut," Caleb explained. "I think if we set one up and find the right frequency, we should be able to contact a dispatcher or an amateur CB buff who can put us in touch with the cops. Not that you've ever cared about what I think, but there you have it."

He was clearly peeved with me, but given the latest development with the thief, I wasn't of the mindset to react to his hostile tone of voice.

"Okay, fine by me. Let's go."

After that, Caleb maintained an uncomfortable silence as we made our way to Radio Hut. He finally said, "Don't worry. I'll have you back to your boyfriend before you even have time to miss him. And though he strikes me as good for nothing, maybe he'll succeed at his mission to free you. God knows I want out of these cuffs as badly as you do."

I briefly considered trying to justify my about-face with Brian, but I had too much pride to kowtow to Caleb's open animosity. I would explain things when I felt good and ready, and not before.

"They're back here," Caleb said as we made our way through Radio Hut's aisles to the shelves that carried ham radios.

"Does it need batteries or anything?" I randomly chose a box from the shelf and turned it over. He leaned over my shoulder to read the instructions. I could feel his breath on my ear.

"Wait," he said in a whisper, holding a finger to his lips. "Did you hear that?"

I heard the distinctive slide-and-click of the cash register at the front of the store. Startled, I sent the radio box clattering to the floor. Oh crap. Caleb and I exchanged alarmed glances. If we were in here with the thief, he was between us and the exit. Rotating his cuffed hand to grab mine, Caleb pulled me toward the stock room. Opening the door stealthily, we slipped inside and softly shut it behind us. No sooner had we leaned against the door than we heard an audible click. Someone had entered the lockdown code into the security keypad reserved only for mall emergencies. We were trapped!

CHAPTER SIXTEEN

Sweet Lord, You Play Me False

Little known fact about me: I'm not cut out for peril. I might have a knack for getting things done, and can grudgingly weather humiliation like a champ, but risking life and/or limb? Not my forte, thank you very much. I spent the summer before my sixth-grade year in a state of almost-constant anxiety after one too many Nancy Drew mysteries led me to obsess over the likelihood of being attacked by a lake-dwelling octopus or getting dumped in an abandoned mine shaft by some ex-con named "Grumper." So needless to say, disbelief quickly gave way to unadulterated panic when I heard the retreating footsteps of whoever it was that had locked us in.

My natural inclination would have been to pace the room—a no-go with the maze of cardboard boxes stacked floor-to-ceiling in our midst, not to mention the impediment chained to my wrist. He and I stood glued in silence to the cement floor, giving my rapid-fire pulse an opportunity to ease up a degree. We each separately took stock (no pun intended) of our fluorescent-lit surroundings, which seemed eerily crypt-like. In addition to the aforementioned boxes, there was a beat-up black file cabinet with the initials W.S. scratched on its front, a "bend at the knees before lifting" safety poster, and a life-sized cardboard cutout of Tom Hanks holding a volleyball. Random. I made a mental note to check the mini fridge later, even though it was grimly affixed with a sticker that read "Abandon Hope, All Ye Who Enter."

"Well, *that* happened," Caleb said after a long silence. Apparently sensing my anxiety, he added, "If he were going to do anything to us, he would've done it already. I don't think he'll be back."

"I hope you're right. But after seeing what he did to Mike, I'm not so sure. What if he decides he wants to take me for his captive bride and ferrets me away to some dilapidated mountain compound far from the world's watching eye?"

"Are you kidding me? Don't flatter yourself."

"Well, excuse me for having a perfectly natural freak-out response to all this. Unlike you, I do not have the emotional detachment of a cyborg. Anyway, what do we do now? No one has any clue we're even here."

He jiggled the door handle, to no avail. Oh brilliant.

"Really?" I said. "The doorknob? That's all you got?" He turned to me looking fed up.

"As a matter of fact, yeah. So what do you suggest, your eminence? By all means, do enlighten me."

Both his question and his sarcasm hung heavy in the stale stockroom air. I didn't really have a plan either; no cunning quick fix, no brilliant tactical maneuver, no ingenious trick up my sleeve . . . other than to make like a girl and scream bloody murder.

"Someone helllllp!" I started wailing in desperation, pounding my unshackled fist against the metal door. "Let us out!!!"

It didn't take long before Caleb joined forces with me, kicking at the door with his steel-toed boot while we both pounded our fists until our hands ached and our throats were raspy.

"This is pointless," he finally said. "No one's down at this end of the building. We might be locked in here until the mall opens back up and a new shift comes in."

"And with 'Arctic Doomsday' out there, who knows when that'll be!" As I succumbed to exhaustion, hunger, fear, and anger, tears started to well up in my eyes.

"Jeez, just calm down, alright?"

"Quit telling me what to do!!" I screamed. "We should have listened to Grady and gone back to the food court, but no—you just had to run off and play hero! Ineffectually, I might add!"

"Ohhhhh." Caleb smacked his free palm to his forehead in an overexaggerated gesture of insight. "Now I get it. Worried he'll think you're ditching him, huh?"

"Who? Grady?"

"No, your scumbag boyfriend. '*My life hasn't been the same without you!*!'" he said, mimicking me. "I've witnessed some pathetic girls in my day, but that display took desperation to a whole new level. I mean, how many more ways will the dude play you before you have the sense god gave a hedgehog to see through his crap?"

"He has yet to get me trapped in a glorified broom closet by some hardened criminal, so you've got a leg up on him there!"

If I was ticked before, his words had now launched a perfect storm of anger. I'd had every intention of trying to explain to Caleb the circumstances with Brian so that he wouldn't think ill of me, but what was the point? He'd already made up his mind about me, and it wasn't a flattering depiction.

"I can't believe I was actually starting to buy into your act." As he said this, Caleb kicked the metal door once more for good measure.

"What 'act?'"

"The one where you claim to give a damn about anyone other than yourself. The one where you pretend to be a normal human being—not the high-and-mighty prima donna we're all supposed to suck up to." So I was right! He *did* think I was a superficial bitch! This whole time I thought we might actually be forming an unorthodox sort of friendship, he'd really just been judging me, solidifying his opinion of me as some "popular girl" cliché. "You and Brian deserve each other," he said with a sullen snarl.

"Go to hell."

"By all means, ladies first." He held up our fettered arms to make his point.

"Why are you being so hostile?"

"Look, I don't have to waste my breath insulting your most beloved Brian, or turning him into some supervillain. He does a good enough job of that all on his own."

"Yeah? You're digging a pretty sizable hole for yourself right now, too." Caleb switched from his default averted glances to look me squarely in the eyes. The only thing worse than having to listen to his aspersions was being physically unable to turn my back on him—or walk away completely.

"If you had any self-respect whatsoever, you'd never give him a second thought," he continued. "Sadly, you can't see that your own self-loathing is what keeps you so emotionally dependent on that deadweight reprobate."

"I don't know about all your psychobabble, but I definitely know dead weight, because I'm looking right at it. I may be stuck in here, and I may be stuck to you, but I'm not required to acknowledge your presence, no matter how long we're trapped together. So consider this the last of our discourse."

"Gladly. After all, I'm sure ignoring peons is what you do best."

And with that, an uncomfortable silence reigned.

***

I'm not sure that people ever really change, but maybe the light in which we perceive them does. How else to explain what I was feeling thirty minutes after Caleb and I had unleashed what I knew would be our last torrent of insults at one another. It wasn't as if that moment, shoving a bag of foam peanuts behind my back, suddenly made him the picture of gallantry. He was still as willful and hotheaded as I could be; a tempestuous soul who navigated his life with cynicism and a paucity of words. But I'd come to realize that when it really mattered he was even-keeled, steady, and solid to the core.

We were back on tentative speaking terms following the crisis-induced bonding moment that had prompted him to take my hand. I still gripped it tightly in mine, taking comfort in his warm grasp. Shifting on the makeshift Styrofoam beanbag chair he'd procured for me, I sighed deeply. My anger with him had subsided, supplanted by the panic and fear of our current conundrum. Caleb's thoughts were clearly headed in the same direction, because he squeezed my hand reassuringly.

"My dad is probably freaking out right about now," I sighed, breaking the silence.

"I'm sure he figures you're safe and sound, just waiting it out here."

"If I'm not home within an hour after my shift, well, let's just say he has the chief of police on speed dial. Which for once would be helpful."

"We'll get out of this, don't worry." His forced optimism was only slightly encouraging. "But you're exaggerating, right? Your old man's not really that strict?"

"I wouldn't call it strict, *per se*—just overprotective. But, to be fair, it's not without good reason."

"Are you referring to your brief but infamous 'criminal' career at Eastern Prep?"

Maybe it was just a delusion brought on by exhaustion and the fact that we'd been attached at the wrists for hours, but even if we never spoke again after tonight, it was somehow paramount that Caleb understood I wasn't the conceited egomaniac he had made me out to be.

"No, actually he's been like that for a long time. Since my mom died."

Caleb was silent; he seemed to be taking it in before responding to my revelation.

"It's like he feels this extra sense of responsibility toward me," I said, "both for my well-being and, I suppose, my happiness. He's constantly trying to make up for what we've both lost—as if an exorbitant allowance and unbridled credit could bring her back. I mean, I adore him, don't get me wrong. But I'm not always sure his overcompensation is what I really need."

"He wants you to have 'all that money can buy'?"

I nodded.

"And I called you a spoiled princess."

"It's okay—I was one, but I've changed my ways, even if it wasn't by choice."

"I'm sorry about your mom," he said. "And I'm sorry about what I said before. It's absolutely none of my business if you want to get back together with your ex."

"Oh my *god*. How could you have possibly thought I would take back that compulsive liar? Don't you know me better than that after everything we've been through tonight?"

"What do you mean? You made it pretty obvious."

"Well, good! That's what I wanted him to believe."

"But you kissed him!"

"*He* kissed *me*."

"Oh great, do you mean to tell me that was just another one of your 'scorned woman' schemes? Because if that's supposed to be revenge, it kind of came across as the opposite."

"No, it wasn't one of my schemes. I mean, not exactly. I would have explained it all to you before now if you hadn't given me the cold shoulder."

"Explained what?"

"My suspicions. Didn't you think it was weird that Brian was in Got Games? Alone?"

I went on to give Caleb my rationale for wanting to keep Brian close. The thought had first occurred to me while my ex was giving me his sob story. He claimed he'd just fallen asleep in an aisle of the game shop. Yeah, right. A more believable scenario was that he'd been playing possum after realizing he'd been caught casing the joint. Rachel and the Itneys had found him bleeding in the jewelry store—what if *he'd* been the one who smashed the glass?

"Oh please, Miranda," Caleb said. "If he's the culprit, then where did he ditch the ski mask Mike described? What about the gun?"

"I don't know. I mean, I can't account for all those details. Maybe it's not a one-man job? Brian could ostensibly be an accomplice or wingman or whatever. All I know is, we can't say for sure where he was during the first two robberies, and that whole story about Lane's Diamonds seems a little too convenient. I know from experience that he's a scoundrel. We can't rule him out as a suspect."

"Slow down a second." A confused smile began to materialize on Caleb's face. "Do you mean to tell me that whole 'hopelessly devoted' routine was just bullshit because you thought he might be the crook?"

"Exactly. How else am I going to get proof if he's involved in this whole thing? And why aren't you taking this more seriously? I mean it's only a hunch, but—"

"Yeah, and a really bad one," he said, his smile broadening. "First of all, I know where Brian was when the computer store was originally robbed."

"Where?"

"He was with me."

"What?!"

"He was trying to coerce me out of *Avalanche X*, like everyone else on the planet."

"Whoops."

"Yeah," he said with a grin. "Second of all, the guy's mommy and daddy clearly don't skimp in the allowance department, what with trips to Aspen, et cetera. It's not like he needs the money."

"Well, I guess you have a point. But—"

"*Thirdly*, he's not exactly a master of deception. I mean, the lines he was feeding you back there would have made a polygraph machine spontaneously combust."

I couldn't help but laugh now, too.

"Yeah, that was pretty bad, you're right."

"*You*, on the other hand, were damn convincing!" He knocked his shoulder against mine teasingly. We were still sitting on the floor, our backs against the door. "I know I was acting like an imbecile—I can't believe I actually thought you wanted him back."

Turning toward him, I playfully furrowed my brow and bumped my forehead against his.

"Jane make Tarzan angry!" I teased.

"More disappointed than angry," he said, before adding almost under his breath, "and maybe a little jealous."

Caleb jealous of Brian? My forehead was still touching his. My stomach fluttered as I looked down at our hands clasped together. He leaned even closer. Then, to my surprise, I did, too. As our lips drew near I realized I'd subconsciously anticipated this moment from the time I'd first I'd laid eyes on him in the blustery parking lot. On paper, there was absolutely nothing about this guy that was my type. I would never have chosen him for myself in the carefully ordered universe I curated. And yet here we were, connected by fate, circumstances, and these strangely serendipitous handcuffs. I'd spent so much of the night reviling him, and yet there was something about his strong and stoic confidence; the way his biting wit could keep pace with mine, the way he seemed to reside somewhere above the fray of petty adolescence . . . those intense eyes . . . that deep voice . . . the unduly modest rock-n-roll hottness. . . .

My body felt electric as I anticipated the inevitable sensation of his lips on mine, and I could have heard a pin drop in that moment. Unfortunately, I ended up hearing something far more strange.

Caleb reared back from me with a surprised look on his face, releasing both my hands.

"Is that what I think it is?!?"

CHAPTER SEVENTEEN

Untie the Spell

The angst-ridden lyrics of a '90s-era grunge rock ballad sung in an off-key warble wound their way into the stockroom where Caleb and I listened in rapt silence, hardly daring to believe our ears—and our good fortune. Unless our captor had a secret penchant for bad karaoke, I had a feeling we were about to be rescued. Jumping to our feet, we threw ourselves at the door, launching a no-holds-barred, repeat performance of our earlier strategy: pounding our fists and screaming at the top of our lungs. The singing halted, midchorus, but the distorted electric guitar track played on, empty of vocals. A voice called out from the other side of the door.

"Miranda? What the—is that you?" Caleb and I teetered between hope and impatience as disorganized chaos seemed to reign in the store proper for nearly a minute. "Hang on, we just need to override the lock. Give me a sec." It seemed like an eternity, but finally the door clicked and swung open. I fell into the sweet certainty of freedom, which took the shape of a guy wearing a giant fuzzy brown monkey costume, complete with elaborate face paint and giant primate ears affixed to his head.

"Mr. Cheezy!?" Caleb and I both exclaimed.

"No, that's Cory, my coworker," said a familiar voice, stepping forward to show his face.

"Colin!" I shouted. "Thank god you're okay! We were worried sick."

"About me? Something's a little wrong with this picture considering you two were the ones screaming for help, and, wow," he glanced surprisingly at our arms, "you never found the key to those handcuffs?" His clown makeup was by now streaked across his face; a bedraggled mop of clown hair poked out from his shirt pocket like an orange handkerchief.

"Where on earth have you been? We've been looking all over for you. Are you okay?" Caleb said.

"Sure, why wouldn't I be? Cory and I just came from the movie theater where we were hanging with a dozen or so other mall employees, including the ladies from Infinity Homewares. (Coolest broads ever, incidentally.) They convinced the projection operator to give us a free film festival and all the popcorn we could eat." He stretched his arms over his head and yawned. "If I don't see another car chase for a month, it will be too soon. Since the weather's still crap, we decided to kill some more time with the karaoke machine. But enough about me, how did you guys end up here? Were you playing 'three minutes in a closet' or something?"

"Uh, no." I laughed and hoped I wasn't blushing, "We were in here to pick up a ham radio and ended up getting locked in by the burglar."

"You rescued us, dude," Caleb added.

"That's crazy! You mean he's still in the mall? Still robbing stores? Man, that's ballsy." Colin looked over his shoulder nervously.

"Oh, it's a full-fledged Agatha Christie novel around here tonight," I replied. "While you guys were kicking back watching Hollywood thrillers, we've been living one. Speaking of, we should grab the radio and head back to the food court. Ariel's probably issued an APB by now."

***

We arrived back at base camp just in time to intercept our own search party. Grady had advocated for staying put, but Ariel and Chad had finally dragooned him into authorizing an "elite team" that included the two of them plus Seth and Troy. We quickly filled them in on our recent adventure, wherein the rent-a-cop launched into a full-on "I told you so" rant. The bellyaching about our having disobeyed his orders trailed off when Caleb showed him the radio we'd appropriated.

"Not a half-bad idea," he grudgingly admitted. "But I'm not sure how it'll help. Even if we manage to reach someone, they'd need a dogsled team to get to us. I'll set it up and see if I can get anyone on the wire. But I hope I don't have to tell you again to quit wandering off. You're real lucky you didn't get hurt."

Once Grady had walked out of earshot, Ariel shot me a concerned look.

"What?" I said, confused. "I'm fine. Don't act so freaked."

"No, it's not that. Brian was here looking for you," she explained. "He said to tell you he was still trying to find a pair of bolt cutters. He seemed . . . well, he seemed under the impression that you two were back together." She glanced from me to Caleb and back again. "Mistaken, I'm sure. . . ."

"Oh that," I laughed uncomfortably. "It's a long story, but he's delusional. Though if he were able to get these off," I jangled my wrist, as if impersonating the ghost of Jacob Marley, "it wouldn't be the worst thing in the world."

Right on cue, Raj materialized next to me with a smug, 'I know I'm awesome' grin.

"Speaking of," he said, "I think we might actually have a solution to your bondage dilemma. I took the liberty of assigning my crew the task of figuring out how to get your handcuffs off. After some brainstorming, they arrived at a few potential solutions—"

"Yeah, one of them involved setting off a homemade explosive," said Derek, his voice dripping with sarcasm. "Maimed beyond recognition, but hey, free of those cuffs!"

"—only one of which is actually viable," Raj said while throwing Derek the stink-eye.

Alfredo was sitting cross-legged on the floor nearby, painting the nails of Dinah, the pastry chef from Just Desserts. He clucked his tongue critically and shook his head.

"Girlfriend's never going to go for it."

"Why would you say that?" I said. "Is it dangerous?"

"Shhh. . . ." Ariel grabbed my free hand and stroked it soothingly. "Let me break it to her."

"Consider my curiosity piqued. What is it?"

"The suggestion was to smear your arm with . . . leftover french fry grease," she blurted out.

"Gross," I said, shuddering. "That's revolting."

"I told you, she won't do it," Alfredo said.

"But it's the only feasible option," Raj said. "Caleb's wrist is too big, but yours just might manage to squeeze through."

"She doesn't even like to look at that stuff, let alone touch it," Ariel said, looking at me with sympathy. "It's never going to work anyway. Sorry, Raj."

"Now wait a sec." I squared my shoulders and lifted my chin indignantly, remembering the way Caleb had earlier labeled me a prima donna. "What's the harm in a little semi-congealed french fry grease if it will get these handcuffs off?"

"That's what I hoped you'd say." Raj had his crew spread some newspapers on the Hot-Dog Kabob counter alongside a can of the offending grease, which he proceeded to apply to my shackled arm.

I couldn't hold back an "Ew," but otherwise, I remained reasonably calm, considering. Caleb stood next to me watching the theater of operation.

"It smells disgusting," he said.

"It feels even worse than it smells!" I said, cringing.

"It could be a lot worse." Ariel was trying to make light of the situation. "It could be congealed mystery meat from the Chinese buffet."

Raj mimicked how I'd need to contort my thumb and wrist, and after a few attempts, I was able to wriggle free to resounding cheers all around.

"My arm feels as light as a feather," I said, letting it float up, level with my shoulder. I glanced at the handcuffs still dangling from Caleb's wrist. It was strange to think that after all these hours stuck together, we were now free to go our separate ways. Was I imagining it, or did the look on Caleb's face reveal the same mixed emotions I was so desperately trying to hide?

"I can't believe it worked!" If I hadn't known Ariel better, I would think she seemed almost disappointed at having been proven wrong. "How does it feel to be liberated?"

"Kind of disgusting, but also pretty great." I was more glib than I felt.

"C'mon," she said, "why don't you get cleaned up and then you can give me the full scoop on what happened with Brian."

"Uh, I'm going to go see if Grady needs any help with the radio," Caleb said, backing away. "You and Ariel are probably long overdue for some 'girl' time."

"See ya," I said, hoping I didn't sound too forlorn.

As I stood alone in front of the bathroom sink wiping the grease from my arm, I relished my newfound freedom, yet I couldn't help but notice a strange sense of loss—something akin to a phantom limb. I thought back to the moment in the stockroom when Caleb had been about to kiss me and I had wanted him to.

Had I just been overwrought or was I actually starting to have feelings for him?

***

Ariel found it hilariously entertaining that I had, if only for a brief amount of time, considered Brian a suspect. I was regaling her with the story and explaining how I'd developed my acting chops (playing *Streetcar's* Blanche DuBois in sophomore year theater), when Chad and Caleb ambled over to report that Grady hadn't been able to make outside contact over the radio.

"So what do we do now?" Ariel said.

"We either wait for this guy to hurt someone else. . . ."

"Or we take matters into our own hands," I said, finishing Caleb's thought.

"But we can't do anything without knowing who *or where* the guy is," Chad said, thumping a fist into his palm.

"I've been thinking. . . ." I said slowly. Caleb and Chad gave each other mock "uh oh, here she goes again" looks. "What about the security footage? Maybe there's something there that would give us a clue."

"Sorry," Grady said, approaching us. "You're about five steps behind me. That's the first thing I checked, and there was nothing to go on. This guy is a professional."

"But what if you missed something?" I said. "You've been down here since Caleb and I got locked in the storeroom. Maybe we ought to go check and see if there's any sign of him on the camera feed from Radio Hut."

"Even if we saw him lock you in, it wouldn't give us any idea as to his whereabouts now," he said, exasperated. "I've told you a dozen times, we need to stay down here and out of this guy's way."

"Caleb and I could go check it out while you keep an eye on everyone," Chad said.

"No more Scooby Doo adventures," Grady said, flushed to his roots. "I said we stay here."

"Look, man, no offense, because I know you're doing your level best to keep us safe, and I respect that," Caleb said. "But what are you prepared to do to stop us?"

Grady considered the question for a minute, his arms crossed over his chest. I knew him well enough to predict that when push came to shove, not even an expert in origami would fold faster.

"Fine," he said. "If you guys insist on playing gumshoe, then I'm going with you. No more civilians are going down on my watch." Normally, I would've cracked a joke at Grady's cop vernacular, but I was grateful to him for wanting to "protect" my friends when I knew being out in the mall with an actual criminal kind of scared the bejesus out of him.

"What about everyone else?" Chad asked.

"They'll be fine down here," Grady said. "You two would be more at risk out there on your own. Besides, I know how to operate the playback system. It will be faster with me there."

"Thanks, Grady," I said, giving him a hug of encouragement.

"Well, you're not giving me much of a choice, are you?" he said. "Chad, Caleb, meet me in five at the foot of the escalator."

I hid the fact that I was a tad *verklempt* as we bid farewell to the boys by joking about reconnaissance missions.

"Watch your back, and cover your wingman," I said, hugging Caleb tightly.

"Ten-four. Roger that."

Ariel, on the other hand, was visibly upset and warned a blushing Chad to be "über careful." He leaned down to give her a kiss on the lips whereupon Caleb and I, realizing somewhat belatedly they were having what is generally deemed "a moment," turned away to give them some privacy.

"Promise you'll come straight back," I said to Caleb. "Find out what you can and then book it back here so we can figure out a plan together. Don't go rogue or anything."

"Sure," he said. "After seeing you in action all night, I'd be a fool to leave you out of any planning. Besides," he said, "I haven't quite given up on us as a package deal."

"Okay, let's do this," Chad interrupted before I could ask Caleb to clarify his cryptic comment. As they headed toward the escalator to meet Grady, Caleb turned to wave back at me, handcuffs hanging from his arm. Why did I feel absurdly as if *my* arm were still attached to the handcuffs? Was it some sort of posttraumatic stress disorder symptom?

"I can't believe we wasted our time talking about Brian when *this* was happening, you little PDA coquette!" I accosted a glowing but flustered Ariel as soon as the boys and Grady crested the first floor. "Details. Spill them. Now." I was dying to know the sequence of events that had led Chad and Ariel to be all blatantly kissy-face. Hoping her story would prove a distraction to us both as we waited for the guys to return, I grabbed her hand and led her over to where Alfredo and Dinah were camped out on a plaid wool blanket. They were waiting for their polish to dry, reading *Cosmo* dating advice aloud to one another in fake British accents, an activity they eagerly tossed aside to join our impromptu gossip session. "Tell us evryfink, luv," Alfredo said to Ariel in mock Cockney, patting a spot next to him on the blanket.

My coworker giddily explained that she and Chad had been lovedrunk virtually from the moment Caleb and I had left the food court following the concert.

"Oh, Miranda, it was incredible!" she said, her naturally pink cheeks flushing almost fuchsia. "He told me he's been crushing on me for months but was too shy to come out and say anything!" I thought back to earlier when Chad had approached me on my break. Oh god, what a dolt I was! He wasn't trying to ask me out—he'd been soliciting my advice for asking out Ariel! Considering Caleb and I had emerged from the stockroom incident unharmed, it was probably a good thing we were out of the picture for a while—it gave Chad a little time to make his move.

"He kissed me when we were in the photo booth. We were just goofing off, taking some silly pictures, and then it happened. . . ." As Ariel confided in us, I could tell by the far-off look in her eyes that it had been her first kiss—and a stellar one, at that. "He called me 'sweet' and 'perfect.' I never even dreamed this was something that could happen. I mean, he could go out with any cheerleader or gorgeous girl that he wants to, but instead he wants *me*!"

Her eyes were dewy, and I could see the little one was overwhelmed by her joy.

"Oh Ariel, *you're* gorgeous. Of course he would want you!" I said, on the verge of crying now, too. In addition to being beside myself with excitement for her, I was wistful, too, wondering if my own future would ever include a romance this good and sincere, unfettered by the trouble and turmoil I'd come to associate with dating.

"It's my birthday wish come true," Ariel said before sighing in happy contentment. "Those candles I blew out must have been enchanted."

"Speaking of," said Dinah. "How'd you enjoy the ice cream cake?" Alfredo and I concurred with Ariel's rave reviews. "Did you let it stand on the counter for a few minutes to thaw a bit, so it'd be easier to cut? I told Grady to mention that to you."

"Actually," I said, a little confused. "It was already half-melted by the time Grady delivered it."

"What?" Dinah looked perplexed. "But that's impossible. I'd just gotten it out of the freezer when he came. It was rock solid. It couldn't have melted in the five-minute walk back to the food court."

I shrugged my shoulders.

"Maybe Grady had to stop somewhere else before he dropped it off here," Ariel said. "He seemed pretty busy in the aftermath of the computer store break-in."

"Nooo. . . ." Dinah shook her head slowly, as if thinking back on the exchange. "He came by to pick up the cake a few minutes after eight."

"Before the computer store got wiped out," I said. "That doesn't make sense. He dropped off the cake at nine, just like I'd asked him to. And I bumped into him running down Main Street about twenty minutes earlier. Why would he have picked it up from you so early, and what did he do with it?"

"Beats me," Dinah said with a shrug. "Though he did seem a little distracted when he came by the bakery. He had a hammer with him. Said he'd been trying to crack the ice that had built up around the door to the loading dock."

The visual of shattered ice made me instantly think of the smashed glass display cases in the computer store. I jumped to my feet in a panic.

"No!"

"What's wrong?" Ariel said, standing up to join me.

I couldn't believe that I'd failed to see it earlier: His agitation following the first robbery. His Chesire Cat–like comings and goings throughout the night. His insistence that we all stay confined to the food court. His convenient failure to make contact with anyone on the shortwave radio.

"Grady's the thief," I said, feeling a cold dread spread over me. "And Caleb and Chad have no idea."

CHAPTER EIGHTEEN

'Tis a Villain, Sir, I Do Not Love to Look On

The peculiar thing about courage is that you can more readily summon it forth when something (or someone?) you love is at stake. Neither Ariel nor I took a moment's pause to consider the jeopardy we were putting ourselves in by going after the guys. Grady's M.O. was pilfering cash and pricey merchandise—but he also wasn't above resorting to violence if anyone got in his way. The fact that Caleb and Chad didn't suspect Grady in the least served as their best protection against him. Still, I wasn't about to stand idly by knowing they were out there alone with the crooked mall cop. Certainly Caleb and Chad could take the scrawny security guard in a *mano-y-mano* struggle. But Grady was armed and, well, there was no telling what he might do if confronted.

"Whatever you do, don't let on that we know anything," I counseled Ariel as we approached the far end of the mall. "We'll just act like our curiosity got the better of us. Grady's used to my wandering ways, though he'll probably be annoyed."

"I hope they're all right!" Ariel said. "I finally got the man of my dreams only to lose him two hours later. This is the most bittersweet love story since *Titanic*!"

"On second thought, you'd better let me do all the talking. Anyway, I'm sure they're fine. Just play it cool. We can explain everything to Chad and Caleb once we get away from Grady."

The inside of the empty security office was depressingly bleak. The only art *per se* was a dartboard studded with darts and a faded "wanted" poster featuring grainy black-and-white photos of people who'd bounced checks, presumably circa a time when people actually wrote checks. A crusty, ancient Mr. Coffee Maker gave off the pungent scent of burnt Folgers, and a ratty, taped-up office chair on wheels sat in front of a bank of six surveillance screens trained on various areas of the mall's interior. Every ten seconds or so, the screens would automatically switch to a different area of the building: the interior of Cheeze Monkey . . . the food court . . . the kiddie playland . . . the dining room at Teasers.

On the desk in front of the monitors, a pale green, sticky slime sat in a coagulated puddle, and I could see that some of the liquid had earlier dripped onto the linoleum floor below.

"Here's where he stashed your birthday cake while he was robbing the jewelry store," I said. "He must have thought the cake would serve as his alibi." Ariel was naturally concerned with far more pressing details.

"They said they were coming here to look at the surveillance footage. We didn't pass them on our way. Where are they?"

"I'm not sure, but I don't like it," I said. We stared for a moment at the security monitors. Apart from our food court posse and a smattering of teenagers still camped in front of the entrance to Worthington's, most of the areas the cameras spied upon were as deserted as a playground on Christmas morning. It was strange to view the mall from this vantage point and to be reminded that, at any time, whoever was on security detail could be watching our every move.

I didn't know the first thing about operating the surveillance system, but Ariel's gamer fangirl background gave her the wherewithal to figure out how to switch screens and zoom in and out.

"Nothing," I said after a few more minutes of scrutiny. "We don't have time to just sit here and wait for them to magically appear."

"We could head over to Worthington's and see if anyone's spotted them down that way?" Ariel said.

As my mind grappled with my next move, my eyes vacantly settled upon an exterior shot of the building. Aside from the top half of a few hedges and a covered bus stop that I recognized as being located on the eastern side of the building, the image was a white blur. Specs of white moved across the screen—the snow was still falling, but only flurries now, not the giant flakes that had bombarded me this afternoon. I narrowed my eyes and tried to focus on the unblemished expanse of snow that occupied most of the monitor.

"See that top right screen?"

"The one looking outside?"

"Yeah. Can you zoom in any more?"

"Sure. But there's nothing there. All I see is snow, and a lot of it. No wonder we weren't allowed to drive home in that!"

She clicked a few keys on an ancient looking computer keyboard, and the screen turned completely white with an up-close shot of the snowy expanse.

"Don't you see it?" I asked.

"See what?"

"Look closer, bottom left." Ariel leaned her face close to the screen.

"Footprints?"

"I can't think what else it would be. And the way it's spread out, it's not just one set."

"It's still snowing," Ariel said, "Which means—"

"—those footprints are fresh!"

***

Based on the location of the bus stop, it was easy to figure out that the tracks were heading straight toward a utility door that led to the kitchen at Teasers. We hightailed it downstairs and started off in that direction, agreeing en route that there must be an innocent explanation for the boys' change of plans. We just had to figure out a way to get to them before Grady suspected that anyone was on to him. I was still having a hard time wrapping my head around the fact that "Officer Doughnut," as he was occasionally called, could be the culprit.

"It's not completely adding up," I said as we sprint-walked down the corridor. "He wasn't carrying any of the loot from PC Pro when I bumped into him around the time of the robbery there."

"Where exactly did you see him?" Ariel pressed.

"At the corner near that kids' clothing store, Rockin' Tots . . . which is right across from—"

"—the door that leads to the loading dock!" Ariel and I were on the same wavelength now. "He must have just dropped off his stash there and was booking it back to his office to get his 'alibi,' my cake!"

"The jewelry store incident happened after I sent him to go look for bolt cutters. No wonder he didn't have any luck. He'd been otherwise occupied during the concert!"

"What about Mike? Why tie him up in the janitor's office if all he wanted was to rob the place?"

"I remember seeing Grady down by Treasure Hunt when I arrived at work, but you're right. Tying up Mike seems a bit extreme for someone who's trying to stay under the radar."

By now we'd reached the far side of the mall where my Eastern Prep classmates had originally encamped. It had thinned out considerably since the helicopter flyover-turned-dance party. More than half had absconded to the food court for the Drunk

Butlers concert, never to return. What few people remained down this way had long since abandoned Teasers and were zonked out on cots and in sleeping bags inside the entrance to Worthington's. Keeping our eyes peeled, Ariel and I crept past the vacant faux-wood hostess stand at the "fine dining" establishment and immediately heard the sound of raised voices coming from the back end of the open kitchen. The restaurant's bustling epicenter usually gleamed with white subway tile and sparkling stainless steel cookware, but it now seemed dark and desolate in the absence of overhead lighting.

My comrade and I scurried into an oversized u-shaped booth with high privacy walls. Crouching ourselves under the table as if in a foxhole, we could just make out the sound of Grady's voice. He'd dispensed with his "aw, shucks" colloquialisms and now assumed an almost diabolical tone of voice.

"Who do you think they're going to believe? It's my word against a bunch of teenage hoodlums," we heard him say. "Besides, no one—apart from the two of you—has any inkling I'm the guy. I slipped up in covering my tracks once, but it won't happen again. That's why I brought you down here."

It was instantly, upsettingly clear that Caleb and Chad had stumbled upon the truth of Grady's guilt, though I wasn't certain how. I couldn't see what was happening, but I had a lucid enough mental picture to realize the situation was heading due south. Holding my breath, I strained to hear the continuing conversation coming from back near the dishwashing station.

"Why'd you do it, Grady?" Caleb's voice was measured and unfaltering. "Why tonight, with so many people still in the mall?"

"Chaos breeds opportunity. The po-po can't respond on a night like this, and I'm surrounded by dozens of other would-be suspects. You kids have done enough looting tonight on your own that, frankly, my crimes don't even seem that out of place."

"Borrowing a few things to pass the time hardly equates to ripping off diamonds, computer equipment, and cash register tills," Chad said. "And none of us beat anyone bloody, come to think of it."

"Scratches," Grady said. "But don't worry, pretty boy. Your face will be spared. Too bad I cut the phone lines earlier tonight, huh?"

"Why do I get the feeling tonight's string of robberies isn't your first rodeo?"

"Well, aren't *you* on the ball?" Grady said. "It's true; I got sprung from the big house about two years back after doing a stint for check fraud."

"Now you've moved on to fencing stolen goods. *En garde!*"

"Go ahead, joke," Grady said. "That's what they all do. You think I'm not aware of all the clever nicknames you punks have for me? The humiliating pranks? The endless ridicule? The spitwads thrown down at me from the upper floor? Everyone just thinks I'm some joke, some loser. I've put up with it my whole life."

"Yeah, you and the millions of other people who got teased at recess. Boo-hoo. Getting picked on isn't what makes you a loser. You're a loser because you never figured out how to get over it." Typical Caleb. His blunt response likely wasn't going to help matters.

"This badge may not have ever earned the respect it deserved, but maybe a loaded weapon will."

"Doubtful." I cringed inwardly. *Caleb, just shut up!* "But if you were really as good at your 'moonlighting gig' as you seem to think, you wouldn't have had to tie up Mike in the janitor's locker room. Are you contemplating branching out into kidnapping?"

"No, idiot." Grady seemed even more on edge now. "It was never part of my plan until he struggled with me and yanked off my ski mask. Stashing him out of sight was a bit of improv—until I could figure out what to do with him. Although I wouldn't have had to resort to such extreme measures if I'd known that hitting him in the head with that bowling trophy would give him partial amnesia. But enough with the running commentary. I don't owe you any explanations. No more talking."

"Seems the damage is done," Caleb shot back. "You've just spilled everything to us." Grady let out a laugh that seemed gravely unbefitting the situation.

"You really don't think I'd allow you to go to the authorities after this, do you?"

Ariel shot me a nervous glance. I knew she was expecting me to "pull a Miranda" right about now, but to be honest, I didn't know what to do. Charging a gun-toting ex-con didn't seem like the most prudent option.

"If you shoot us, everyone next door at Worthington's is going to come running," Chad said.

"Oh, but I'm not a *killer*. At least, not in the sense of someone who would ever get caught. Now oblige me by stepping into the walk-in freezer so we can conclude this nasty business."

"Hate to break it to you pal, but you've tried this tactic on me already," Caleb said. "It didn't work."

"The stock room at Radio Hut wasn't kept at minus-ten degrees. And you don't have that little tease, Miranda, to help keep you warm."

"You leave Miranda the hell out of this!"

"Maybe I will and maybe I won't. She's certainly complicated what should have been some pretty cut-and-dry loot boosting.

But I wouldn't worry about her or that little Twinkle Toes she calls a friend. You'll have a lot more to worry about when your bodies enter a state of profound hypothermia. You've heard the saying: Revenge is a dish best served cold? Rest assured, I'll return periodically to check on you, and when I see that you've finally cashed in your chips, I'll drag you out to a nearby snowbank. 'An unfortunate weather-related accident,' they'll all say."

Ariel gasped, but I placed a reassuring hand on her shoulder. "You don't want to do this," I heard Chad say before the freezer door slammed with a thud.

CHAPTER NINETEEN

Hark! Now I Hear Them—Ding-Dong, Bell

Had we not found the three of them when we did, Chad and Caleb might have been goners, but luckily, I knew we could fetch the guys from the freezer as soon as Grady left. I thought back to the game of chess Caleb and I had played earlier that night as I planned my strategy for freeing them, trying to think a few steps ahead. Grady would come unglued the minute he realized Chad and Caleb were missing, and we had to be prepared for his next move—but first things first.

I brought my fingers to my lips, signaling to Ariel that she shouldn't move a muscle, and willed myself to be patient. Grady was still poking around the restaurant, and we both crouched lower to avoid detection. After a few minutes, the room grew quiet, and I slowly emerged from underneath the table, reasonably certain the coast was clear. Ariel was about to follow my lead when we heard a clattering from in the kitchen. Instinctively, I bolted on tiptoes to a nearby hall leading to the restrooms. (Thank god the floors were carpeted!) Ariel remained stranded under the table, when to my horror, Grady sauntered into the dining room casually holding a beer in his hand! He took a seat at a table only seven or eight feet from where Ariel crouched, and his back was to us as he sipped contemplatively from his bottle. If he so much as glanced around the room, he could hardly miss my barely concealed coworker. I stared in agony at my friend adrift out there in Grady's midst, wishing I'd been gifted with the power to make her invisible.

From what I could tell, Grady seemed absorbed in his thoughts—it was now or never. I beckoned from the hallway for Ariel to make a run for it, but she just stared back at me with eyes like saucers, paralyzed with fear. I motioned to her again, more insistently now, prompting an ever-so-faint sound that filled me instantly with dread.

"Ding-ding-ding." As Ariel shook her head vigorously in refusal, she'd inadvertently triggered the high-pitched knell of the dainty bell earrings that hung from her lobes. Things had just gone from bad to catastrophic.

Grady was instantly on his feet, nabbing Ariel by her spindly elbow before she could make a break for it.

"What are you doing here?!" he said, enraged, while shaking her like a snow globe.

"Nothing! I was just, er, sent down here to score some Grey Poupon. All we have is that bright yellow stuff, and the gourmands were revolting."

"You were looking for mustard. . . ?"

"Uh-huh!" Ariel gave one of her award-winning grins, a desperate-but-valiant effort.

"Under the table. . . ?"

"Yeah! Well, no," Ariel said, fumbling for words. "I lost my earring right around here, and oh—here it is! Duh! Well, I'd better be going, so—"

"Not so fast. Miranda would never have sent you down here alone."

"Actually, Miranda didn't send me. She's been fast asleep behind the Hot-Dog Kabob counter for the the last forty-five minutes or so. Poor girl's had a long night." My heart was in my throat realizing that she was trying to save my butt. A more loyal friend could not have existed. Unfortunately, Grady wasn't buying it.

"She's here, you brat, isn't she? Tell me where she is!" His back was still to me, but I was sure that within seconds, he'd be upending the place trying to find me. If I got caught, we'd all be SOL, and standing here in this dead-end hallway wasn't going to protect me for much longer. There wasn't time to deliberate or hatch a plan. I just had to act, and fast. While Grady continued trying to shake the truth from Ariel, I slipped sight-unseen toward the kitchen, heading straight for the walk-in freezer.

With as little sound as possible, I opened the door to Caleb and Chad's cold crypt, holding a finger to my lips to warn them that silence was critical. As I whispered Ariel's perilous circumstances, they locked eyes and, without words, seemed to form a joint plan. Then, like a commando in an elite Navy Seal team, Caleb motioned Chad forward and indicated that I should follow them.

The miscreant was still giving Ariel the third degree when they tackled him from behind. Caleb grabbed Grady's gun from his waistband and pointed it at him while Chad bear-hugged him to the ground. (Seems I didn't give football players enough credit!) Everyone in the room was panting for air by the time Grady was pinned face-down with the business-end of the pistol pointed firmly against his skull.

"What do we do with him now?" I said. "It could be hours—or longer—before we can finally get the authorities here."

"We've got to lock him up somewhere." I could see it was an effort for Chad to keep the struggling captive restrained as he said this. I fretted over the possibility that Caleb might actually be tasked with using the gun on Grady if he managed to break free, and I was fairly certain Grady would be willing to call his bluff.

"Do you think there's any rope or a chain somewhere around here to tie him up with—at least until we can figure out a better solution?" I scanned the dining room. A more vindictive person might have suggested putting him in the freezer like he had planned to do with Chad and Caleb, but that option was off the table. If I'd learned one thing today, it was that justice was always preferable to revenge.

"Miranda, you'll have to go to Camperville and try to find something that'll work," said Caleb. "They've gotta sell some climbing rope—strong duct tape might even hold. Something to keep him immobile until the *real* cops can get here."

"No way. I'm not leaving you. We'll find something here."

"Hey, guys—" Ariel said.

"Dude—quit wriggling if you don't want an elbow in your face," Chad warned Grady. He wasn't going to be able to keep him pinned much longer.

"Hey, guys—" It was Ariel again, but I was onto another idea.

"If we could get those curtains down off the rod, we might be able to use them to truss him up . . . the fabric's a little thick, but—"

"GUYS!!!!!" Ariel's voice silenced us all, even Grady, who'd been taunting us and grousing this entire time. "Why don't we use the handcuffs?"

"No way am I letting Caleb get chained to this guy," I replied.

"Great idea, babe," Chad smiled up sweetly at his girl. "But we can't get even get the handcuffs open."

"We don't have the key," Caleb said. Ariel glanced nervously at both Caleb and me, a rueful smile wavering tentatively on her face.

"Well, maybe we do." She lowered her chin and fished one hand into the deep pocket of her jumper. I stared in astonishment as she produced a small silver key.

"YOU!!!!" Chad, Caleb, and I were a weary trio of slack-jaws. "When did you find the key?"

"Have you had it all along?" I said.

"Guilty as charged," Ariel said, hanging her head sheepishly.

"Why on earth—?" I was majorly confused and slightly peeved. Being played by my prep school cohorts was one thing, but I'd never suspected it from the girl I considered my tried-and-true friend. Please let her have a good reason for deceiving me like this.

"I'm so sorry, Miranda. Caleb, you, too," she said, hurrying over to him to release him from the manacle. Caleb slapped one of Grady's wrists in the cuffs, then ushered him across the room to the salad bar, to which he affixed the other end of the steel shackles.

"We've been trying to find a way out of these all night," I admonished her. "Why did you do this?"

"I wanted to give you a taste of your own medicine. And I mean that in the best way possible."

"I'm not in the mood for aphorisms. Cut the crap and explain yourself."

"Oh come on, Miranda! You're always pulling strings behind the scenes, setting the universe spinning along whatever orbit you dictate. So sue me if I decided to tie your hands for a while . . . and play matchmaker."

"Say what?!" While I attempted to wrap my brain around her explanation, Caleb had started to softly chuckle.

"Oh, man," he said with a laugh. "She totally stole a page from your playbook."

"Oh, you think this is funny?"

"Yeah, actually, I do," he said, hiding his grin with his fist.

"Matchmaker?!" I turned back to Ariel. "What makes you believe that yoking me to *this* yahoo would somehow make us fall hopelessly in love?"

"Seeing is believing." Ariel wrapped her arm lovingly around Chad's waist. He kissed her affectionately on top of the forehead. "As a matter of fact, my plan worked out even better than I'd expected it to. You guys are perfect for each other, whether you want to admit it or not."

I crossed my arms in a demonstration of defiance and stormed off a few paces to brood—and blush.

CHAPTER TWENTY

We Are Such Stuff as Dreams Are Made On

Leaving Grady securely handcuffed in Teasers to await dawn and his punishment, we headed back down an empty Main Street toward the food court. The others were amped-up and giddy, eager to fill in everyone else on our white-knuckle adventure. But when we arrived at base camp, it was eerily quiet, as if a spell had been cast over the once-bustling epicenter of our night in captivity. The lights were dimmed and I immediately noticed that the rest of our informal bunch had hunkered down in makeshift bedrolls, finally too exhausted not to yield to slumber's succor.

"Should we wake them?" Ariel said as we trod noiselessly over our snoozing chums.

"Not now," I said *sotto voce*, pulling a fleece blanket emblazoned with neon-colored handprints up over Alfredo's shoulders. "It's so peaceful."

Chad walked over to our retinue of supplies from earlier, shuffled around for a bit, and then, in the dim light, headed back to us.

"There are only two pillows and two blankets left," he said in a low voice, beginning to spread them out on the floor. "You girls go ahead and lie down for a few hours. Caleb and I can tough it out."

"No way!" Ariel said, stifling a yawn. Sleep had begun to beckon us, thanks to the darkness of the food court and the intensity of our night-long ordeal. "Chad, sweetie, you take one pillow and I'll snuggle with you. We'll share a blanket." Wow, for someone who'd never even gone on a date before, she'd adapted to her new role as girlfriend like a seasoned pro. Good for her, though it admittedly felt strange that the idol-worship she once reserved for me was now being lavished on someone else. The little lark had up and left the proverbial nest, a fact that made me feel proud, but not without some poignancy. Ariel looked my way as if urging me to make a similar sleeping arrangement offer. I glanced at Caleb warily, not sure what to say.

"It's all right," he said, letting me off the hook. "You've been stuck with me for the last eight hours. I'd say you paid your dues. I'll be fine over here." He took a seat and leaned back against a nearby wall, folding his arms and stretching his legs out before him. He closed his eyes, and I stared at him for a moment, admiring his strong jawline and that adorable cleft in his chin. The nerves in my body seemed miffed that he was five feet away instead of the five inches that had separated us for most of the night. I missed matching my gait to his, the protective security of his stalwart presence, and the reassuring touch of his hand in mine. The faint sound of breathing and soft snores could be heard in the room, and I knew Ariel and Chad were off in cuddle heaven under a table near Fro-Yo-Yo across the room. I sat up from my pillow and glanced at him again.

"The floor's really cold." His head was still tilted back against the wall, but at the sound of my voice his eyes perked open to look at me, quizzically. I waited for him to say something, but he only nodded his agreement and closed his lids again. Damn it. I'll need to try another gambit.

"Your back might get all jacked-up sleeping against the wall like that." He didn't even open his eyes this time.

"I'll be fine." He either couldn't take a hint or he was having fun making me beg.

"Well, umm, it's a pretty big blanket—meant for a king-sized bed, I think. Maybe we could draw an imaginary line down the pillow and split it or something. Like you said, we've been together all night. A few more hours isn't going to kill us."

As if capitulating, he gave a knowing smile and slowly got to his feet. I wriggled my head to the far end of my pillow and threw open the down comforter to give him entree to our little cocoon.

Relieved to have him back by my side—or maybe just too tired to care about appearance's sake anymore—I snuggled against him and drifted off to sleep, a storm-tossed skiff now safely in harbour.

***

"Rise and shine, campers! Shake it off! Wake up! Wake up!"

Groans, coughs, and a distant, "But I don't *wanna* go to school!" roused me from my warm slumber. I rolled over sleepily, my eyes still closed, and felt a warm breath on my face. Huh?! Caleb startled and blinked, seemingly as surprised as I was to find himself waking up next to me. The food court's fluorescent overhead lights were back on now, and with my lids at half-mast, I surveyed the scene.

The court was a sight to behold—you'd have thought we were the last remaining survivors of a postapocalyptic wasteland. Tables and potted plants were overturned. Food and condiments had been splattered, Jackson Pollack–like, across most of the counters. One of the red plastic trays had (god knows how) lodged itself in the fancy crystal chandelier, and "The Mariner" had been filled to overflowing with used plastic cups and straws—if we'd accomplished nothing else last night, we'd at least managed to drink our weight in soda.

Our food court manager, Randall, was walking through the mess in his boots and winter parka, gently nudging some of the deeper sleepers awake.

"Up and at 'em, guys," he said, kicking a few of the errant wheeled janitorial buckets out of the way.

"What time is it?" Riley asked, unwittingly displaying an epic case of bedhead. I died a little inside wondering what kind of national disaster I must have resembled.

"It's quarter to nine," Randall said. "We've got a plow and a crew with shovels out in the parking lot right now extricating the cars."

"You mean we can go home?" Caleb said, still reclining on his elbow under the blanket.

"Soon. They plowed and salted most of the main roads, but the secondary roads are still pretty hazardous. They're predicting warmer temperatures today, which should help. You guys were wise to stay put last night."

"As if we had any choice," Troy said.

"Yeah, well, you were a lot safer in here than out there."

I threw the blanket off my legs and got to my feet. "You wanna bet?"

"Oh, hey, Miranda!" Randall made his way over to me. "Don't worry—a few guys from the maintenance team were the first to make it in this morning, and they found Grady—along with your little note spelling out all his crimes. The police are down there questioning him now."

"Oh, what a relief! I was worried he'd sweet-talk his way out before we could explain the situation."

"Apparently, he tried, but from what I've heard upstairs, there's evidence in his office as well as down by the loading dock where he'd stashed the stolen goods. But I'm sure they'll want to question everyone who was in the mall. I'm going to head down that way and find out some more details."

Randall trudged off and, after flashing me a quick grin, Caleb stood up, clasped his hands, and stretched them overhead with a yawn. Now that I had a chance to suss out the room, I was surprised at how many of the Eastern Prep kids had migrated to our little enclave over the course of the night. They say a crisis brings people together, and while I liked to think maybe I had a little something to do with it (what with conjuring dance parties, promoting rock concerts, and all), I guessed it was probably due to the fact that the food court had more bathrooms.

Ariel came flitting over to me like a cygnet from *Swan Lake*. Was she always this perky after two hours of sleep, or was the carton of OJ in her hand spiked with an energy drink? I suspected the former.

"You're not *really* mad at me, are you?" she said, pausing to gauge my reaction.

I thought about everything she'd done for me last night, gamely going along with my every whim, no matter how vainglorious, silly, or even dangerous. I'd initially made the excuse that I'd done it as a diversion for her, when all along she'd been the one trying to help *me*.

"How could I be mad at my best friend?"

"I'm your best friend?! I've never had a best friend!" I half-expected her to implode into a maelstrom of confetti, but instead she leaned in closer and whispered for my ears only. "Would you say I did a good job, then?"

I glanced at her, attempting a look of nonchalance even though I knew exactly what she meant.

"We can talk about it later."

Once the rest of us managed to catch up to Ariel's level of alertness (well, maybe not quite), Caleb rightfully pointed out that it wasn't fair for the janitors to have to deal with our super-sized mess. He and Chad rounded up some empty garbage bins with Colin and Cory while Ariel and I teamed up to put the tables to rights and wipe them down. Ours wasn't the only cleanup effort in progress. Raj's crew circled around the Itneys like mad scientists, deliberating a solution to their orange-hued, henna-stained skin, with suggestions ranging from boric acid to WD-40.

"But I kind of like it," Whitney said. "It's like the ultimate fake tan!"

I had just tossed Ariel a spray bottle with disinfectant when I felt a light tap on my shoulder. I turned to find Rachel standing behind me with her arms crossed. Uh oh.

"Rumor has it you were the grand architect of my elevator run-in with Bunnicula," she said, her eyes narrowing.

"Oh. Uh . . . yeah. I guess that wasn't exactly the most mature thing in the world to have done, but—"

"Forget it. My therapist has been telling me for months that exposure treatment was the only thing that would cure my *leporiphobia.*"

"Come again?"

"That's the scientific name: the paralyzing fear of bunny rabbits. I'm sure it wasn't your intention, but you probably cured me. Anyway, that's not what I wanted to talk to you about."

"Okay?" I thought the situation between us had mellowed after our encounter in the ladies' room, but now I wasn't so sure.

"I think you might need to have a word with Brian."

"I'd prefer not to. Why are you telling me this?"

"He's outside like a raving lunatic right now, spelling out 'I Heart Miranda Prospero' in the snow."

"You've got to be joking."

"I wish. You can see it from the upstairs atrium overlooking the parking lot. Of course, he forgot the 'S' in your last name. Please tell me you are not back together with that sleazebag. I know you and I didn't end on great terms, but I think I speak for us all," she pointed over to the Itneys, "when I say that we can do better than him."

In so many ways, Rachel and I represented two very opposite sides of the same coin, but on this point we were in agreement. I'd cried too many tears at the mere thought of my ex-boyfriend over the course of the last month, and though I had vilified him for the mess he'd made of my life, I could see in hindsight that I was to blame for being so uncomprehendingly spellbound by him in the first place. It was just as Caleb had said to Grady; I hadn't just been a fool for dating Brian, I'd been a bigger fool for not figuring out how to get over him. Suddenly, I felt unable to suppress my laughter at the visual of Brian tromping through the snow to profess his love when we all knew it would melt as soon as the mercury climbed. Tears welled up in my eyes, but this time, they stemmed from the kind of unimpeded laughter that gives you a complete ab workout. It seemed a fitting enough reprisal that he was pining away for me in a mad state of unrequited love, literally left out in the cold for a change. Who knows? Perhaps it would make him a better person. After all, that's what it had done for me.

I reassured Rachel that I was in no danger of reconciling with Brian and headed back to Hot-Dog Kabob to grab some fresh towels. Truth be told, I had spotted Caleb in the vicinity and hoped to intercept him for a quick *tête-à-tête* before we all made our exodus. Worried the enchantment had somehow faded now that the night had officially ended, I needed to know that Caleb still had a "package deal" in mind for us. He'd been bewitched—or so it seemed—by my prevailing sovereignty in this inconsequential mall microcosm. Yet now that I'd decided to put my plotting and politicking behind me, I wondered if what remained would still be of interest to him. Who was the "great and powerful" Miranda Prospero now that I had abdicated my reign of petty payback? I was standing behind the counter parsing all this when Reggie and Stacy, the Eastern Prep kids who'd taken such joy in heckling me mere hours ago, approached. Ariel skedaddled over and lifted the counter to stand by my side, as if worried I was about to face an encore rationing of insults.

"Is it true?" Stacy looked at me quizzically. "Were *you* the one who brought down the mall cop?"

"Well, it wasn't just me."

"She's being modest," said Ariel. "Grady would've gotten away with murder—literally—if it hadn't been for Miranda."

"Way to go, Ace." Reggie offered his hand to me.

"Weren't you terrified?" Stacy looked spooked.

"I, uh, didn't really have time to be."

"I bet the big shots at corporate will give you a mega-reward or something," Colin said as a crowd began to gather. "The financial implications of catching him are pretty huge."

"Score!" Troy said, leaning over the Spitfire counter to join in the conversation. "You know what that means, Miranda—you'll be able to quit your job. Which, sorry to be selfish, will suck, big time, for me."

"Oh, Troy! I almost forgot. A copy of *Avalanche X* turned up for the little dude. Remind me before you take off—I'll get it for you."

"Seriously? This is going to make that kid's decade! You are a lifesaver, Miranda. See what I mean?" Troy looked around at the dozen or so who'd assembled around us. "She's a cross between, oh I don't know, Lara Croft and," he paused to consider and then blurted out, "Mother freakin' Teresa!"

"She's hardly Mother Teresa." Caleb had appeared at the edge of the crowd. "At least, I *hope* she isn't."

I wasn't sure how to respond to this. I was so used to peppering him with cynical comebacks that any other approach made me feel tentative and uncharacteristically shy.

"So . . . do you think you will? Quit your job, I mean?" Ariel looked as sad as a bent-winged butterfly as she posed the question.

"Yeah." The crowd parted as Caleb nudged his way through. "Would you blow this fast-food stand for good?" He stood before me and my heart leaped in response to his lopsided grin. I knew I'd found something that elicited far more thrill and excitement than any of my sundry schemes, and I could tell by the glimmer of admiration in his eyes that he felt the same.

"What, and miss out on fashion like this?" Relinquishing the last vestiges of my former snobby self, I reached under the counter again, this time pulling out my once-dreaded wiener-propelled hat. I placed it proudly on my head and turned to Ariel with a wink. "Help me?"

"Sure thing!" Her braces gleamed as though they'd just been Windexed. Looking at this kindred spirit, I felt a pang of gratitude in recognition of her unconditional friendship, even when I'd once been only condescendingly tolerant of her. I was lucky to have her. She arranged the hat on my head, tucked under a stray wisp of bang, and then murmured, "You're good."

She meant my hat, I think. Or did she? I thought back to the note my mom had jotted down in the margin of my book: "*Rebuke = redemption!*" It had seemed like English major b.s. the first time I'd seen it, but strangely, I could appreciate its significance now. I'm not going to pretend that tumbling off my perch on the elite high school pedestal hadn't hurt. I wouldn't wish my recent experience on anyone. Yet had I not fallen (or been unwittingly pushed?) out of so-called favor, I would never have ended up here, among these fascinatingly funny, steadfast, authentic, plain-old *wonderful weirdos* that I now called my friends. I glanced at Caleb. Not exactly a Jane Austen hero, but still. He'd taken me to task at times throughout the night, but his challenges seemed rooted in the belief that I was capable of more. Whether he'd intended to or not, he'd brought out the best in me, and I wanted more than anything to show him that I had learned from all my missteps. If real life truly did mirror the game of chess, now was my golden opportunity to, like the all-powerful queen, change course. It was time to make my move.

I gave Ariel's shoulders a quick squeeze, then popped up the hinged counter and walked right into the waiting arms of Caleb. The crowd dispersed—or at least, I didn't notice them anymore—as he enveloped me in a tight bear hug. I looked up into his face and was rewarded with a tender kiss on the forehead.

"You know, the first time I saw you, you were wearing this hat," he reminded me, playfully spinning its propeller. I brushed aside his bangs and then stood on tiptoe to plant a reciprocal kiss on his lips. As I gave in to the spectacular awesomeness of the moment, I heard a noise as if from far away. I leaned back and turned to look. Still surrounding us were all our new friends, wolf-whistling, cheering, and clapping. I blushed and flashed them an I'm-so-busted grin.

It finally dawned on me that I didn't necessarily have to give up *all* my influence and stratagems—that was part of my charm, after all. I made a silent vow to use my talents only for good—and I knew a couple of people who'd make sure I stayed true to that resolution. I grabbed Caleb by the wrist, pulling him in the direction of the escalator.

"Where are you taking me?" he asked.

"To Got Games for a pair of those trick handcuffs," I said. "I'm not letting you get away so easy this time."

As we headed up the escalator, I looked back down at the food court spread out below us in all its garish glory. In some ways it had been, for at least one night, an island unto itself; the promise of its time-worn theme fulfilled beyond measure. I waved farewell to the sea of faces about to be released from their confinement and said a silent goodbye to the past. My vision began to swirl, dreamlike, and I blinked back the hint of happy tears, wondering if the food court and everyone in it might vanish completely. Caleb's arm tightened around me and I knew it was no illusion. A bright new day awaited us, and I hoped for smooth sailing ahead.